Here Come the Grooms!

Romance is definitely in the air, as we take the plunge into the sea of matrimony. Get swept up in the excitement, as five very different couples prepare to tie the knot. Not all is as it seems, however, some nasty surprises bring heartache and uncertainty. Will everyone get the happy ending they deserve?

Four Weddings and A Scandal!
Copyright©2017 Jimi Goninan
ISBN 978-1-911478-10-2
Cover art and design by Dawné Dominique

Published by
Lydian Press 2017
Find us on the World Wide Web at
http://www.lydianpress.com

CONTENTS

FOUR WEDDINGS AND A SCANDAL!

Jimi Goninan

Lydian Press

For my beloved husband, Antoine.

Without you, none of this would be possible.

A MATTER OF TRADITION

Torquil MacBeth drummed his thick, masculine fingers in a nervous fashion on the white linen covering of the bridal table. His stomach churned slightly, as he gazed out at the crowd on the rooftop terrace of the Grand Babylon Hotel. A light, pleasant spring breeze began to ruffle the pieces of white paper before him, causing Torquil to quickly place his right hand upon them, to prevent them from taking flight. He'd be completely lost without them, as the pages contained the speech he was scheduled to give in a little over fifteen minutes. Public speaking was unquestionably one of his least favorite things in the world, but as the best man for the wedding of his brother, Hamish, it wasn't like he had much of a choice.

Why did I agree to this? I need to man up and stop stressing. Besides Mom and Dad will kill me if I don't.

As a firefighter, he'd enthusiastically rushed into burning buildings on a number of occasions without half the amount of trepidation he felt at addressing an expectant crowd. In search of a distraction, Torquil focused his attention onto the several good-looking waiters wandering about the spacious terrace; in particular, the way their cropped black jackets drew attention to the pert little asses beneath.

I'd love to rip down their trousers and squeeze right in between those tight…

Feeling a familiar tingling in his loins, Torquil switched his attention back to the happy couple, lest his kilt begin to betray his lustful thoughts…his manhood wasn't terribly easy to hide when it hardened to its full nine inches.

His fellow firefighters would have gotten a kick out of seeing him sporting a kilt, although Torquil had no intention of showing them the wedding photos. His fiery head of hair and famous last name already made him the target of merciless teasing and he had no desire to give his co-workers further ammunition for their friendly fire. There had been no torment, however, regarding his sexual inclinations, as the station enforced a strict no-tolerance policy on such outdated attitudes. That aside, he was a popular and well-valued member of the crew.

Despite his Scottish heritage, Torquil wasn't as blue-white as some of his relatives but was still pale by a normal beachgoer standard. Even so, his fair complexion didn't stop him from attempting to sun himself at Murdoch Beach at every opportunity, taking great care to slather himself in cream to avoid ending up looking like a lobster. Like his brothers, Torquil was of a tall stature, topped with strawberry blond locks that tended towards a deeper auburn in their facial hair, although Torquil was the only one of the three to have a full beard. Due to the strenuous training and demands of his profession, Torquil was also the most well-built of his siblings, an unmistakable fact given the way his solid frame was squeezed inside his traditional wedding attire.

Most aspects of Hamish's wedding to his childhood sweetheart, Fiona, had followed custom, primarily to please their elder relations. Both families hailed from Scotland, but had moved to Port Davinica after the Second World War; and carried their traditions with them across the seas. The kilts they were all sporting, for example, were in the MacBeth family colors – red, green and blue, with lines of yellow. Also in homage to the clan, the bride's gown was trimmed with the same tartan around the hem, coupled with small, yellow flowers woven into her hair. To finish off the look, the men were all wearing a sporran on a silver chain, knee-high white socks, white crisp dress shirts and tailored black jackets.

Even though Torquil had enjoyed the ceremony – apart from the bagpiper, which had sounded like the plaintive wails of a dying tone-deaf cat – he had long ago resigned himself to not being of the marrying kind. Not that there hadn't been one or two potential candidates over the years but it had always ended in heartbreak. These days, the prospect of getting his needs met by an array of talented men held infinitely more appeal than settling down with just the one.

Looking down at his watch, Torquil noted that it was almost time for the speeches, meaning that he needed to go and fetch the special bottles of champagne he'd dropped off with the event coordinator earlier in the evening. Standing up, Torquil shoved the pages of his speech into his sporran and strode purposefully across the terrace.

Pity I can't drink an entire bottle to myself before the speech. Enough time for that later. Besides, nobody likes a sloppy, drunk speaker.

* * *

As he approached the large oak bar located on the far left of the terrace, Torquil's eyes were caught by the attractiveness of both the barmen on duty.

The waiters and the bar staff! Do they only employ models here? Their uniforms are so sexy…especially the bow ties.

One was a twinkish blond with boyishly handsome features, while the other, swarthier gent appeared to be slightly older, in his early-thirties, with dark inviting eyes. Even though Torquil wouldn't have said no to bedding either of them, it was the darker of the pair that had really piqued his interest. His muscular build highlighted by a tight-fitting white button up shirt that appeared to be straining to keep the barman inside.

Goddamn! I wonder if the lower half matches?

Deliberately moving to the side of the sultry barman, Torquil waited patiently as he finished serving other guests, admiring the way the sleeves of his shirt strained enticingly as the muscles beneath went about their work mixing drinks. Lost in a pleasant daydream, Torquil's nerves about giving the speech had all but disappeared. A minute or so later, it was his turn to be served.

"Hi. I'm the best man. I arranged for a few particular bottles to be put away for the toasts and I was told that I needed to tell someone about ten minutes beforehand."

"Sure, I can organize that for you."

The barman flashed Torquil a winning smile that showed off his brilliant white teeth and caught the attention of Torquil's cock. There was a slight accent to the barman's words that only served to add to his allure. Torquil hazarded a guess that the barman was Brazilian, given his caramel-colored skin and dark features.

"Thanks…" Torquil looked down momentarily to read the barman's name off of his badge. "Joao."

"My pleasure, Sir."

There was a seductive tone to Joao's voice, combined with yet another warm smile, which caused Torquil to wonder what else might give him pleasure. The pair held eye contact for a smidge longer that politeness would seem to dictate, but neither party seemed inclined to put an end to their interaction. Torquil felt his pulse quicken slightly and suddenly found himself unexpectedly tongue-tied.

"OK…great…thanks again…see you later, then."

And with that Torquil quickly made his way back to the bridal table, desperately hoping that his face hadn't flushed pink in embarrassment.

"See you later, then." What the hell was I thinking? Why did he have such an effect on me? It's probably just my nerves about the speech.

As he sat back down, Torquil risked a look back towards the bar and saw that Joao was engaged with other guests and apparently not aware of his gaze at all. Annoyingly, he felt more than a little disappointed that the barman wasn't looking back.

Do I really need an ego boost that badly? Best stick to perving on the waiters, or focus on that damn speech. Erghhh, I wish it was already over.

* * *

As promised, the bottles arrived promptly at the table ten minutes later, although to Torquil's slight dissatisfaction it was the blond barman who was the one to bring over the alcohol. Radiating professionalism, the waiters then went to work ensuring that the champagne was quickly distributed amongst the guests' glasses.

Realizing that he could no longer delay the inevitable, Torquil took a big swig of the champagne before him, before standing up and moving over to the small wooded lectern just to the side of the bridal table. He took the microphone in hand and cleared his throat to summon the attention of the crowd. His palms were sweating profusely and his heart thumped uncomfortably fast in his chest. Taking one last deep breath, Torquil looked down at the pieces of increasingly damp pages in his left hand and began.

"Hi, everyone. For those who don't know me I'm the groom's brother, Torquil, and it gives me so much pleasure to be here, on this very special night…although with so much tartan it looks like a casting for Braveheart 2 out there."

A small ripple of laughter spread through the crowd, allowing Torquil to relax ever so slightly. His grip on the pages of the speech became less tense and he felt the hint of a smile upon his lips, as he plowed on with his speech.

Lame joke but at least it worked.

Five minutes later, Torquil was smiling widely. Not only was he nearing the end of the speech but the crowd also seemed to be enjoying his words – well, they weren't booing him at any rate.

"Now, please raise your glasses high and join me in toasting the new Mr. and Mrs. MacBeth!"

There were many murmurs of agreement, as people echoed the toast and lifted their glasses. Sitting back down, Torquil was pleased to see Hamish and new wife looking at him with matching regards of happiness.

Since he'd gotten through his speech without incident, Torquil felt the stress beginning to leave his body, allowing him to properly relax for the first time since he'd set foot on the terrace and begin to really enjoy the rest of the proceedings. During the other speeches, Torquil's eyes kept traveling back in the direction of the bar and towards the handsome man working behind it. Beneath his kilt, his manhood twitched, as thoughts of what the barman may look like out of his snug hotel uniform and lying spread-eagle on Torquil's bed downstairs.

This isn't the place. That's right; the shower would be better. Stop it! Focus on Hamish and Fiona, it's their day. I can find hot bartenders to fuck any other day.

Reluctantly, Torquil turned his gaze back to his brother who was just finishing up his own speech.

"And I can't tell you how grateful I am that you've all come here to support me and my beautiful fian…*wife*, sorry that might take a little while to get used to." The crowd tittered at the gaff, as Hamish continued on. "And I'd like to especially thank my baby brother, Torquil, who has been such a help in getting everything together for this amazing day. OK, enough mushy stuff. Drink up!"

There was a rousing chorus of concurrence, as the guests sipped their champagne in celebration. Torquil felt his face heating as he blushed at his brother's words and looked away, inadvertently locking eyes with Joao who was gazing directly at him in return. Suddenly, feeling even more tad self-conscious,

Torquil looked down but could still sense the barman's eyes upon him.

Busted! But maybe he wants the same thing as me? I'm such a hopeless cockhound.

* * *

Thirty minutes later, Torquil was trapped in a most dire situation. He had been wandering around mingling with the guests and had gotten stuck chatting with his mother's lifelong best friend, Daphne, a rotund woman with kindly features and graying raven hair done up in a chignon.

This is torture! I'm never going to get away. Maybe I could fake a seizure?

"Yes, Stephan had such a wonderful time in Europe but now he's back and I think he's looking to settle down," prattled Daphne, who was not very subtly trying to set Torquil up with her son. "If only he could meet the right man."

"Yes, it can be tough," agreed Torquil, in as a non-committal tone as he could muster.

"Maybe you both could catch up for a drink sometime? You two were thick-as-thieves when you were little. I was just talking about that with your mother earlier."

I bet you were. Why can't mothers help themselves from interfering in their children's lives? They're so wasting their time.

It wasn't that he found Stephan unattractive, quite the opposite. Stephan possessed a powerful footballer build, ruffled sandy-blond hair and sharp green eyes, which all went together to form quite the stunning combination…but it wasn't to be. Unbeknownst to their parents, several years beforehand Torquil and Stephan had already had an ill fated one-night-stand, after quite a few drinks, where they discovered that they weren't sexually compatible in the slightest. They had remained on friendly terms but it was perfectly clear to both gents that there could never be anything more between them.

"Yeah, I might give him a buzz." Torquil's tone sounded insincere to his own ears but that didn't appear to deter Daphne.

"I'm sure he'd *love* to hear from you!"

Just then Torquil was saved from further awkward conversation by a loud 'pop' and a wetness running down the left side of his shirt, he'd left his jacket resting on the back of his chair, and onto his kilt. Angrily, Torquil turned to the source of the unexpected moisture only to find a very remorseful-looking Joao standing there holding a half-empty bottle of champagne. Torquil's annoyance faded at once and he found himself standing there dumbly while Joao burst into a flurry of apologies.

"Oh, I'm so sorry, Sir. This never normally happens. Please forgive my clumsiness."

He can spray me any time.

"No, it's OK. Accidents happen," reassured Torquil, in a calm, even timbre. "No need to worry about it."

"I really hope I haven't ruined your skirt...sorry kilt." Joao frantically dabbed at the Torquil's clothing with the white tea towel he'd been carrying. "We should put water on it straight away so that it doesn't stain."

"I'm sure it'll be fine."

"Please, Sir. Come with me and I'll help clean you up."

At least I get to escape this conversation. Maybe the gods are looking out for me, after all?

"Well, if you insist." Joao turned briefly back to his mother's best friend. "It's been a pleasure, Daphne. I'll chat to you later."

Taking the lead, Joao directed Torquil to a small passageway to the right side of the terrace, which in turn led to a wooden doorway at the end.

"It's the staff bathroom," explained Joao. "Far less busy."

Don't see why that matters to clean the stain but I don't mind being alone with him.

Closing the door behind them, Joao went to the sink and dampened a handful of paper towels.

"I really am *so* sorry," Joao apologized once more, his eyes full of shame. "I'm not normally so clumsy, Sir."

"It's alright, and you don't have to keep calling me, *Sir*. It makes me feel like an old man," joked the fireman. "My name's Torquil, although you can call me Quil if you like. Besides, you rescued me from having a difficult conversation."

"Then I'm glad…Quil. Maybe I should have spurted on you earlier."

Did he really just say that? Hot with a cheeky sense of humor! Definitely my type.

Evidently taking Torquil's silence as a rebuke the barman apologized.

"Sorry, just a silly joke."

"It was funny," Torquil reassured him, liking the barman even more by the second.

Working silently for the next minute, Joao moved downwards from dabbing Torquil's shirt to his kilt. Sinking to his knees, apparently so that he wouldn't have to bend so far, the barman patted the material dry.

As he gazed down at the barman, all sorts of illicit thoughts raced through Torquil's mind, causing his nipples to harden and his manhood begin to swell.

He does look good on his knees. I have a few other things he can clean for me.

"I really like your kilt," murmured Joao, a coy regard upon his face.

"Thanks." On a mischievous impulse, Torquil decided to toy with the barman. "My PVC one is even better."

"Really? It sounds…hot." His fingers lingered by the hem of the kilt, lightly brushing up against Torquil's skin. "You know I've always wondered whether or not the rumors are true about what guys wear under their kilts." There was a wayward edge to his tone.

The sensation of the fingers resting on the back of his knee sent little waves of pleasure up towards Torquil's crotch. A bead of sweat trickled down his leg, the stuffiness of the bathroom and the closeness of Joao both causing his temperature to rise.

Feeling daring, Torquil made him an offer.

"Why don't you find out?"

Joao looked up and the pair once more locked eyes. The look of lust in Joao's eyes was unmistakable and Torquil bit his bottom lip in a gesture of impious expectation. They held the gaze for a few tense moments before Joao let his left hand slide slowly up under the kilt and along Torquil's muscular thigh. His other hand rested on Torquil's calf in a firm grip, their eyes still connected.

Naturally, Torquil's manhood rapidly stirred in gleeful anticipation of what the handsome Brazilian may do with his wandering hand. Suddenly, the door crashed open and in came one of the waiters from the reception, a tall dark-haired gent with ice-blue eyes, causing Joao to whip his hand free and leap to his feet, and Torquil to take a hasty step backwards.

"Oops, sorry Joao. Didn't know you were... *busy*," said the newcomer, correctly assessing the situation.

"Trent! I...I...I spilled some champagne and was just trying to clean it up."

"I bet you were." The smirk on lips clearly showed exactly what he thought of the excuse. "Service with a smile."

Just then, another of the waiters, a shorter lad with spiky black hair and an impish look about his features, came rushing through the door.

"Have you got it lit yet?"

"Shut up, Matt!" berated Trent.

It was then that Torquil looked down and saw that Trent had a joint in his hand and quickly gathered why both of the lads had been in a rush to use the staff bathroom. Both Trent and Matt had matching looks of guilt and began to babble their excuses at the same time.

"We never usually do this…"

"We're so sorry…"

"Please don't report us…"

Despite their rude interruption, Torquil was feeling magnanimous, seeing he had just been about to do something equally as naughty.

"It's OK, guys. I won't say a word."

"Thanks, so much," gushed Matt

"Yeah, we'll just let you get back to…ummm." Trent raised his eyebrows in a thoroughly suggestive manner, which appeared to have an adverse effect on Joao.

"I should get back to the bar, too," said Joao, sheepishly exiting the bathroom, followed closely behind by Matt and Trent.

Left by himself, Torquil was slightly at a loss. He felt a sticky wetness on his thigh from where his engorged cockhead had smeared precum. Thankfully, his sporran had managed to conceal the semi-aroused manhood underneath his kilt. Even though he was slightly peeved that he'd been interrupted, Torquil gave himself an admonishing look in the mirror.

I shouldn't have been doing that here anyway. What if someone from the wedding had caught us? I should get back to the party and stop letting my cock override my common sense.

Giving himself a once over in the mirror, Torquil was pleased to see that the drying champagne hadn't seemed to stain his outfit. After smoothing a few errant hairs back into place, the somewhat sexually frustrated fireman made his way back to the reception.

* * *

Retaking his place at the bridal table, Torquil watched as Hamish and Fiona danced and laughed together, twirling amongst the other couples on the shiny surface of the polished wooden dance floor. Their happiness was pointedly clear and Torquil felt his lips forming into a large grin. Just then, Hamish looked up and caught Torquil's eye, giving him a big thumbs-up before returning his attention to his new bride.

It must be nice to be so much in love…and for it to last.

Naturally, this led Torquil to ponder his own singleton status...and the relationships that had kept him that way for the past few years. For the most part, he didn't mind being on his own but there was the odd occasion – right now, for example – where Torquil felt a discomforting hint of loneliness.

His first major heartbreak had occurred at the tender age of eighteen, with a completely unexpected betrayal by high school boyfriend, Travis – a solidly-built blond, with mud brown eyes and chiseled features. At the prom after party, Torquil had gone outside for some fresh air and noticed that the windows of his footballer boyfriend's hatchback were fogged up. Upon closer inspection, he saw that the car was moving in a rhythmic fashion, with the sound of muffled groans coming through the door. Yanking open the back door, Torquil was dismayed to discover Travis being manfully plowed by St. Francis Xavier's handsome quarterback. Needless to say, the occupants of the backseat were thoroughly surprised and froze mid-thrust.

"What the fuck, Travis?" yelled Torquil.

"Quil, it's not what..."

"Not, what? So, that isn't Jason's cock in your ass?" Torquil felt himself literally shaking with rage. "And after all those times you wouldn't let me fuck you because you said it was too painful. How long has this been going on?"

"What do you mean? This is the only time," protested Travis, but his guilty expression betrayed the truth.

"Unbelievable! I guess I know what all those late-night practice sessions were about."

"Babe, please…"

"Shut it. I don't want to hear any of your pathetic excuses."

"I should go," mumbled Jason shamefacedly.

"Don't bother, you can have him. Fuck you both!"

"Quil, wait!"

Ignoring Travis' pleas, Torquil raced back inside and proceeded to get astoundingly drunk, sobbing a great deal of the time. It had been a crushing blow and had destroyed all childish notions in Torquil of a fairytale-esque true and lasting love.

Fortunately, his cynicism faded with time and he'd managed to trust again, even enjoying a few good, if short-lived, relationships. Naively, Torquil never thought he could ever feel so betrayed as that first time. And he was correct, until a good ten years later when he'd unexpectedly dropped by the apartment of his fiancé, Benjamin, to pick up his phone that he'd forgotten that morning.

Using his key, Torquil let himself into the apartment, as Benjamin was supposed to be at work. Walking inside the front door, Torquil was immediately hit by the instantly recognizable sounds of sodomy – manly grunts coupled with skin slapping together.

What the hell? That can't be what I think it is.

Torquil stormed down the hallway and into the lounge room where he was confronted by the disturbing sight of ten naked men in the midst of an orgy. It wasn't the orgy itself that troubled him – he'd participated in his fair share – rather it was the fact that his allegedly monogamous fiancé was smack bang of the middle of it, eagerly being fucked from both ends. Benjamin's smooth muscular body was glistening with sweat and his handsome visage was contorted in pleasure. Even worse, Torquil recognized most of the guys from their gym whom they'd both been on friendly terms with.

Far too fucking friendly apparently.

"Benjamin!" The fury in is voice was unmistakable. "What the fuck is this?"

It took a few seconds before his fiancé realized who was calling his name. In a rush, Benjamin extricated himself from the men who'd been using him and scrambled to his feet, looking very much like a trapped animal.

"Torquil, honey. What are you doing here?"

"Is that all you've got to say to me?"

Clearly wanting to escape the argument, the other men hastily grabbed their clothes and fled the apartment in short order.

"Guess I'll see you at the gym, guys," called Torquil to their retreating backs, his words laced with venom. "Thanks for stopping by."

"Please, Torquil. I can explain."

"Really? Explain what, exactly? Explain why you're holding sex parties when we're supposed to be getting married in two months? What the fuck is wrong with you? Does our commitment mean nothing to you?"

"Of course, it does," proclaimed Benjamin, although he couldn't quite meet Torquil's eyes. "I...I...I was just starting to feel pressured by all the wedding arrangements and settling down forever and I...I needed a release. It was just sex, it didn't mean anything, I swear!"

"So, is this why you didn't want to live together until after the wedding? You make me sick!"

Much yelling and begging followed over the course of the next hour but Torquil wasn't moved by his fiancé's pleas and justifications. Breaking off the engagement, he quickly charged around the apartment, snatching up the various belongings that he'd left over the course of their relationship. His bag full, Torquil fled the apartment without a backward glance.

Afterwards, Torquil vowed off serious relationships, content to get his needs met by random strangers and the occasional fuck-buddy. If anything started to even hint at being serious Torquil would pull away and find new flesh to play with instead.

Returning his attention to the present, Torquil took in the festivities before him, but his eyes kept settling on the numerous happy couples spread around the terrace, all appearing to be having such a lovely time.

Am I missing out? Could I find something real? Do I want to risk getting hurt again?

"Everything alright, son?" asked Torquil's father, Wallace, who'd just taken a seat beside him.

"Yeah, I'm fine."

"Thinking about that wanker, Benjamin?"

How the hell does he know? Am I that transparent?

"Dad." An annoyed growl underlined Torquil's voice. "Can we not talk about my failed relationship? It's not about me today, OK."

"Whatever you say, son. But you're much better off without him and I have faith that you'll find that special someone, just like your brothers have."

"Dad!"

"Alright, alright. I'm just worried about you. You'll understand when you have kids of your own." He gave Torquil a firm squeeze on the shoulder and then moved off to join his smiling wife over on the far side of the terrace.

I don't know I'll ever have what they do. He means well, I guess. But he'll be waiting a while for grandchildren from me. I need some space.

* * *

In an effort to shake of his maudlin state, Torquil wandered off to a secluded part of the terrace, behind a row of large potted shrubs, to gaze up at the stars. The night sky always helped him put his issues into perspective given how wonderfully small the sight of all those distant twinkling lights made him feel in the scheme of things, and the knowledge that his problems were nothing but a momentarily blink in the history of time. He had a telescope set up on the small balcony of his apartment and often looked up into the heavens. Opportunely, his apartment was located at the edge of the city facing towards the nearby mountains so his view was less diminished by the light pollution of the city.

Lost in the stars, Torquil didn't hear the approaching footsteps until someone was almost directly behind him. Without a word, the interloper then grabbed a firm handful of Torquil's ass. The thick fingers pushed the material of his kilt into the crease of his buttocks. A surge of excitement flowed straight to Torquil's crotch.

Joao?

Torquil spun around and instead of coming face to face with the swarthy barman, he found himself staring at Fiona's obviously very drunk – and straight – brother, Hans. The telltale odor of whisky wafted off of him and given the way he was swaying from side to side, and his glassy gray eyes, Torquil was surprised he could still stand. Ordinarily, Torquil found Hans rather attractive, with his floppy blond hair, slim build and pleasant features but he certainly wasn't looking his best at present.

"Watch yourself," warned Torquil.

"What? I was just having a bit of fun." His slurred words only served to confirm his overindulgence. "Don't be such a stick-in-the-mud!"

Why me? This is so not what I needed tonight.

"Go have fun with someone else, then." Torquil remarked dismissively. "I'm really not in the mood."

"Come on! Susan hasn't put out in months and I need some relief." Hans moved closer to Torquil, grabbing a firm hold of his own crotch. "So, how bout you help me out and suck my cock?"

Classy. Hope he acts better than this when he's sober.

Admittedly, Torquil had played with his share of horny, drunk straight guys in the past and while they could be fun from time to time, it certainly wasn't what he wanted to do at his brother's wedding. Especially, as he knew that Hans' wife, Susan, was heavily pregnant with their second child and at home on bed rest.

"No, I'm not going to suck it. I'm not interested."

"Why not? I thought all you gays loved it."

Seriously? Didn't think he was that much of a douche. His poor wife.

"You should go, now." Struggling to keep his rising anger in check, Torquil moved backwards away from Hans and closer to the ledge. A malicious idea formed in his mind. "Keep it up and I'll tell your sister. How would you like that?"

The threat had an instantly sobering effect on Hans, who immediately backed away.

"Hey, no need to get nasty. I was just mucking around. Can't you take a joke?"

"Sure, fine, whatever."

Torquil turned away from Hans and resumed looking out over the city, making it obvious that he considered the conversation finished. Hans stood awkwardly beside him for several seconds before taking the hint and leaving.

"Catch you later." Hans grumbled in a belligerent timbre, as he drunkenly stumbled off, leaving Torquil to stare broodingly into the night.

Good riddance.

* * *

Several minutes later, Torquil was once more disturbed by the sound of footsteps approaching him from behind. Spinning around, Torquil began to unleash a furious tirade at Hans.

"Look I already told you, I'm not going to suck you…"

He caught himself mid-sentence, realizing too late that it was Joao and not Fiona's drunken brother.

"Not even if I ask nicely?"

Joao's sweet smile held a promise of delightful wickedness.

"I'm so sorry, I thought you were…it doesn't matter. You must think I'm an idiot."

"No, not at all but I'm guessing your outburst was meant for that blond guy that staggered away from here a little while ago."

"Yeah, the bride's brother. Drunk and wanting something I didn't want to give him. But you probably don't want to hear about that."

The barman edged closer towards Torquil until their bodies were only inches apart. The earlier yearning had returned with full force, Torquil's carnal longings urging him to take immediate advantage of the situation.

"No, not really." Joao smiled seductively. "I saw you pass by the bar earlier and when I got a break I came looking for you."

"For me?"

He's a much better prospect than Hans, but I should still be behaving myself.

"Yes, you, sexy Scotsman," whispered Joao, his words laden with seduction. "If you don't want to suck me, how about just a kiss, then?"

"I'd happily do both if you…"

The rest of his sentence was lost as their mouths came together and kissed furiously, followed closely afterwards by their bodies. Hands latched onto one another, drawing the men into a tight embrace, up against the edge of the sandstone wall. Torquil caught a waft of a musky-honey scent as the barman pressed his muscular body into his even harder.

Nice cologne…or is that his natural odor?

Losing track of time, Torquil's previous malaise evaporated as his thoughts were only concerned with satisfying his urgent need. The minutes ticked by as the twosome ravished one another, their erections rubbing together through the material of the kilt and Joao's trousers. Joao's hands went under the kilt and cupped the bare buttocks beneath, firmly massaging them. Things seemed to be heading in a very naughty direction indeed when suddenly Joao broke away, although it was with an air of great reluctance.

"Mmm...I love kissing a man with a beard. I could do it all night but I have to stop. I'm *so* sorry, I need to get back to the bar." Glancing down at his watch, he grimaced. "And I was due back five minutes ago."

Torquil was seized by a sudden impulse.

I can't let this be it. I need more!

"Do you want to come to my hotel room when you're finished for the night?"

Joao's lips broke into a broad smile that traveled upwards to light up his darkly inviting eyes.

"Thought you'd never ask."

"Room 1003."

"I'll come for you."

"I can't wait!"

Giving Torquil one last firm kiss, Joao turned and walked back towards the terrace. Entranced, Torquil very much enjoyed the sight of the barman's deliciously round derriere straining the material of his snug black work pants. After waiting a few minutes for his erection to stop tenting his kilt, Torquil rejoined the celebrations in a far happier mood than he had left.

* * *

Throughout the rest of the evening, the pair kept exchanging glances across the terrace. Try as he might to fully engage in conversation with his relatives and the other guests, Torquil found his attention drifting back to Joao…and that explosive kiss.

In an effort to pass the time until their rendezvous, Torquil took to the dance floor. His most regular dance partner was his four-year-old niece, Arabella, the daughter of his eldest brother and his wife – Callum and Alisa. In Torquil's view she was the most adorable little girl in the world. He was also rather fond of their other child, Noah, who had been left with Alisa's parents for the evening, as he was only a few months old. A stylish-looking Arabella was dressed in an electric-blue dress with white ballet slippers and a silver ribbon tying her long brunette curls into a sweet plait, all of which complimented her china-doll complexion and inquisitive blue eyes.

Given the late hour, her normally boundless childish energy had been somewhat depleted. The last dance had seen Torquil carrying the increasingly weary child, still moving in slow, side-to-side motions with her head resting against the crook of his neck. Her shallow breaths tickled at his neck, as she drifted ever closer to slumber.

"I've come to relieve you of duty, soldier," joked Alisa, her curvaceous form highlighted by her elegant pea-green gown.

"The poor thing, she's all tuckered out," said Torquil.

"Well she does love dancing with her Uncle Torquil. You're so good with her, maybe you should think about…"

Why does everyone think I need to procreate? Would it be so bad to have a little Arabella of my own?

"Not you, too!"

"OK, OK. Sorry, I remember the pressure well. But it would be nice for Noah and Arabella to have some cousins. You would make a good father, too, you know."

"Thanks for the vote of confidence but I'm not so sure that's where my life is headed. I don't even have the prospect of a boyfriend, let alone kids…unless the stork drops one off."

"Oh, dear," laughed Alisa. "Maybe you should have a talk to your parents about where babies come from."

"No, thank you. I've already spent one exceedingly awkward afternoon in dad's workshop, enduring the birds and bees talk."

I knew more than he did. If only he knew that Travis and I had been fucking for three months by then.

"Besides, I'm sure Hamish and Fiona will be helping out with that soon enough. They're probably at it right now!"

The happy couple had bid farewell to their guests an hour beforehand. Judging by the look upon both their faces, Torquil correctly assumed what they'd had in mind.

"True. But that doesn't mean you can't think about it. As for finding a boyfriend, what about the gorgeous man tending bar over there?" Alisa gestured none too subtly towards Joao, her emerald eyes sparkling with mischief. "He's been making eyes at you all night and by the way you've been looking back I'd say you're just as keen."

"I don't know what you're…"

Ignoring Torquil's half-hearted protest she continued. "You never know where these things will lead. I'd given up finding a decent man until your brother came along and swept me off my feet and right into bed!"

"Too much information!"

The pair laughed companionably together, they'd always enjoyed a friendly relationship filled with gentle teasing.

"OK. I'll go round up my husband." Alisa took the angelically sleeping bundle from Torquil's arms. "And you can go wrangle yourself a dark and handsome stranger."

"I make no promises."

The knowing look that Alisa cast back at him clearly showed how little she believed that.

Around ten minutes later, things were starting to wind down, most of the guests having drifted away in drips and drabs, while the staff had slowly started to tidy up the terrace area. Torquil went up to his parents, who were still slow dancing in the middle of the dance floor.

Would it be so bad to have that again? If only.

"Sorry to interrupt, but it's bedtime for me," said Torquil giving his parents a kiss each on the cheek. "Have fun."

"No stamina, you young'uns," teased Wallace.

"Leave the boy alone." Bonnie admonished her husband good-naturedly. "Goodnight Sweetpea, see you in the morning."

As he exited the terrace, Torquil caught Joao's eye and smiled. He caught the elevator down two floors to his room and anxiously awaited the arrival of the barman.

* * *

Once inside his room, Torquil rushed around picking up all the clothing he'd hastily discarded earlier whilst getting ready for the wedding, and generally tried to make the place presentable. A few minutes later, Torquil stopped to survey his work. Satisfied with the neatness, he made his way to the bathroom and quickly brushed his teeth, before starting to fiddle with his hair, trying to make it the perfect mix of tousled and devil-may-care…a hard feat at the best of times.

It's like I'm getting ready for a date. Why am I acting like a nervous bride? It's just sex…but maybe it could be more. Can't let Alisa get into my head.

Just as Torquil exited the bathroom, there was a firm knock at the door, which he had to restrain himself from running to answer. Opening the door, he found Joao, who was looking even tastier than before, his bow tie undone, as were the two top buttons of his white shirt, replete with a sexy smile.

"Room service." Smirking cheekily, Joao moved forward, pouncing on Torquil, wrapping him up in his arms as they kissed.

No further words were needed as they maneuvered inside, the door shutting with a resounding thud behind them. Joao pushed Torquil pushed up against the solid door as they kissed. Soon both their shirts were wide open and Joao's black trousers and underwear were pooled around his ankles. The passion from the terrace had increased threefold, the privacy of the hotel room allowing them to properly give in to their baser, lust-driven instincts. There was an urgent sense of mutual need, as the lads grasped and clawed at one another. Torquil's senses were in overdrive, his nostrils were filled with the musky-honey scent once more and the sweet taste Joao's kiss caused his cockhead to moisten in excitement.

Suddenly, Joao dropped to his knees and promptly shoved his head under the kilt. Torquil felt the barman's face kissing up his legs, searching for his crotch, which was hardening by the second. Once there, Joao devoured the manhood with a practiced ease, his face rubbing into Torquil's trimmed, fiery-red hair. Torquil groaned as the moist warmth surrounded his cock and the tongue swirled all around his shaft.

Hungrily, Joao went about his work with no gentleness, pausing only briefly in his efforts to suck and tug on the heavy ball sack with his mouth. He milked the member with his hand while suckling at the cockhead, his tongue licking up every trace of the precious salty-sweet precum. Feasting for a good five minutes, his mouth moved from the shaft to the balls and then licked all around the creases, not leaving even a single square inch of the crotch un-tasted.

Apparently not wanting Torquil to blow just yet, Joao stopped his pleasurable assault and ducked out from under the kilt. Without waiting for Torquil to say a word, Joao spun the Scotsman around to face the door, spreading his legs wider, before he bobbed back under the kilt once more. Using his strong hands, Joao spread Torquil's cheeks, kneading the fleshy mounds as he buried his face deep between them. His tongue swirled around the puckered entrance and little by little began to sneak inside.

Pressed up against the door, Torquil was groaning as Joao pleasured his sensitive hole. He reached his right hand back and grasped the back of Joao's head pulling him in even closer. Torquil then felt fingers, as well as the tongue, probing his tight rosebud; leaving him in no doubt as to what Joao was after...and what Torquil was more than eager to give.

Soon after, Torquil heard the telltale crinkling of a condom packet opening. Torquil looked over his shoulder to see Joao rolling the lubricated latex down his extremely aroused looking manhood. It wasn't as long as Torquil's own nine inches but the shaft was much thicker and almost black in color.

Goddamn! He's even bigger than I thought. I'm definitely going to feel that!

Standing up, Joao lifted the kilt, exposing Torquil's pale muscular buttocks. He held the kilt up in his left hand while his right guided his sheathed weapon right to the moist entrance. His white shirt was opened all the way showing off his beautifully well-developed chest and defined abs.

Torquil felt the familiar pressure on his sphincter, as the bulbous head nudged against it purposefully. He tilted his hips back, in order to open himself further and allow the erect manhood easier access. Gasping as the cockhead breached his ring, Torquil was extremely grateful that Joao then allowed him time to adjust before pushing in further. When the discomfort subsided, Torquil pushed back slightly, encouraging Joao to continue.

Taking the hint, Joao grabbed a hold of Torquil's hips and began to slide himself in gently. His thick shaft stretched the passageway, causing a good deal of moaning and squirming from Torquil, who was loudly broadcasting his enjoyment of the proceedings. Joao pushed himself inside until he bottomed out, his balls resting against the round globes of Torquil's buttocks. After a few moments reprieve, Joao began to grind slowly into Torquil, while nibbling the back of his neck and up to the top of his right ear, eliciting even noisier sounds of satisfaction. His hands moved upwards from Torquil's solid hips and roamed over the pale torso, tracing the taut stomach muscles and brushing over the erect pink nipples.

As the strokes started to grow ever deeper, Torquil clawed at the door. The sensation of his ass being worked so capably, coupled with the strong, exploring hands, sent waves of pleasure up and down his writhing body. All of a sudden Joao's hands returned to Torquil's hips and gripped them tightly, before launching into a harsh pounding tempo. The sound of their skin slapping together rang throughout the room, as did Torquil's groans of enjoyment.

Grunting with every thrust, Torquil relished being stretched so completely. It had been a while since he'd been expertly topped and he hoped that their sexploits would continue for quite some time. The ferocious hammering of his passage was mixed in with gentle loving pumps, which only served to transport Torquil to a higher plane of ecstasy. After a while, Joao took pity on Torquil's poor abused ass and pulled out. The twosome resumed their passionate kissing from before, disrobing each other as they stumbled towards the bed.

Falling down to the mattress, they soon twisted around into a greedy sixty-nine. Torquil got his first taste of Joao's impressive manhood, teasing the head with his tongue before gulping down the thick shaft, corkscrewing up and down until the untamed bush at the base tickled against his nose. His hands wandered over Joao's smooth buttocks, his fingers creeping into the crease and working their way inwards to the hairy hole. As he sucked, Torquil teased the entrance, causing an enthusiastic response in Joao, who, in turn, sucked even harder and reciprocated the light fingering.

Breaking away, Torquil moved off the bed and stood by the side. Torquil reached down and pulled Joao over, so that his head was tilted over the edge and then slowly slid his erection in between the barman's open, inviting lips. Thrusting gently at first, Torquil reached down to tweak Joao's nipples. As the pace increased, he raked his nails over the muscular body beneath him, while Joao's hands held tightly onto Torquil's powerful thighs.

Eager for release, the fireman's hips began to move at a frantic speed, slamming his manhood down Joao's eager throat. All too soon, the load building in his balls was ready for its well-earned discharge. After a quick series of hard thrusts, Torquil sailed over the edge and his thick load gushed into the silky embrace of his companion's mouth.

When he'd sucked down every last drop, Joao released the manhood from the suction of his hungry mouth and pulled Torquil back down to the bed for a long, languid kiss. All of a sudden, Joao moved around and grabbed Torquil roughly, flipping him face down on the bed. Spreading the cheeks wide again, Joao enthusiastically gave another thorough rimming before re-suiting up and slamming back inside the velvety passage. With all the build up, it only took a minute of frenzied pounding before the barman began to shudder with the beginnings of ejaculation. He grunted and shook as he exploded into the condom, pumping until every spurt of seed had been released.

Exhausted, the twosome laid together, holding one another while their breathing slowed to a resting rate. Once recovered, Torquil took Joao by the hand and led him into the bathroom for a leisurely shower. As the hot water caressed their strained bodies, the pair began to gently kiss. Predictably, the kissing soon led to a round of mutual masturbation and the subsequent re-emptying of their ball sacks all over the white, tiled floor of the shower.

After toweling off, they moved back into the main room and Torquil climbed back into the disheveled bed. Instead of joining the fireman, Joao went to the pile of discarded clothing on the floor and tried on Torquil's kilt. He twirled around a few times, letting the material raise up to expose his privates.

"What do you think?" asked Joao cheekily. "Does it suit me?"

In response, Torquil jumped back out of the bed and swept Joao up into an ardent embrace. They fell to the floor, their hunger for one another nowhere near sated. This time, Torquil took the dominant role, after fetching more protection, plowing Joao's eager ass, doggy style at first and then a myriad of positions about the hotel room, defiling a good deal of the furniture in their wake. Sweat dripped off of them, as they consummated their desire, over and over again. The room soon became heavily scented with the aroma of their manly sport.

Retiring to the bed again, Joao laid flat on his back with Torquil straddled over his hips. Torquil took himself in hand and within a minute came across his playmate's face – at Joao's insistence – sending a whitewash across his handsome features. Evidently taking great delight in it, Joao ran his hands over his face, massaging in the cream, before licking it off of his long fingers.

Fuck that's hot!

Looking down at Joao, Torquil was a little overcome by an unanticipated wave of emotion. There was undoubtedly a strong sexual connection between the pair but Torquil had an inkling that it might lead to something more than just a one-night-stand.

Stop overanalyzing! Just enjoy what it is. Best I take what I can now then.

"Would you like to stay the night?" offered Torquil, somewhat uncharacteristically.

"I'd love to!" Joao pulled him down into a deliciously liquid kiss, which went on for some minutes.

Eventually, Torquil hopped up to switch off the lights. In the faint light cast by the moon, Torquil made his way back, his eyes never leaving the strong masculine form spread out on the bed. Even in the soft lighting, Joao's beauty was evident and rather something to behold.

Climbing into bed, Torquil wasted no time encircling Joao in his arms, cuddling him from behind. His companion's musky-honey scent wafted into his nose and Torquil couldn't help but to breathe it in as he pulled the strapping Brazilian even closer in towards him. As the effort of his exertions finally took their toll, Torquil sleepily closed his eyes and soon drifted off into a contented slumber.

* * *

The next morning, Torquil awoke to sun streaming through the hotel window; he'd forgotten to close the curtains during all of his and Joao's nocturnal activities. The thought of what they'd gotten up to made him smile and he rolled over with the intention of having some morning fun when instead of finding a muscular man, his arm connected with only the sheet. Opening his eyes properly, Torquil saw that the other side of the bed was empty, as was the room, his playmate having left at some point during his slumber.

Guess, I shouldn't be surprised. Oh well, it was some unexpected fun at least. It's probably for the best...I don't want to get attached.

Despite Torquil's policy of keeping things light and simple he couldn't help but feel a little saddened...and not just because he'd missed out on morning sex. His disappointment was short-lived, however, as moments later the door to his hotel room opened and in walked Joao with a tray laden with fragrant coffee and scrumptious-looking pastries.

"Thought you might need a little something to eat after all that *hard* work last night."

Filled with a renewed happiness, Torquil promptly sat up in bed and felt a huge grin sliding up his face.

"I'm ravenous, thanks!"

Joao brought the tray to the bed and then hopped in beside Torquil. The pair then enjoyed a leisurely breakfast together, exchanging smiles and the occasional gentle caress. As they ate, there was an idea turning over and over in Torquil's head.

Just ask him. But what if he says no? Don't be a pussy! Do I really want to do this? Here goes nothing.

Summoning his inner courage, Torquil finished his chocolate and almond croissant and sat up a little straighter.

"Do you have anything planned for today?" Torquil tried his best to keep the hopefulness out of his voice.

"Yeah, actually I do."

"Oh, OK." Despite his best efforts, Torquil felt his easy smile fade from his face as disappointment took hold.

"I'm spending it fucking you."

In a fit of delight, Torquil moved forward to give Joao a series of steamy kisses. Putting the tray to the side, the two came together, their passion once more ignited.

Thankfully, Torquil had a late check out and they managed to leave the room after only two more rounds of excited play. When Torquil finally made it downstairs to the lobby he said a quick goodbye to his family members, while Joao waited for him downstairs in the hotel car park – neither of the pair particularly in the mood for awkward introductions.

Thirty minutes later, the twosome was naked again in the privacy of Torquil's apartment. Clothing wasn't even a vague option for the rest of the day, as they spent their time rolling around together – fucking off and on with the occasional break for sustenance and easy conversation.

Man cannot live on cock alone!

As night fell, the lads were seated on the balcony, with Joao wrapped up in Torquil's arms as they sat peering up at the stars. There was a comfortableness between them that Torquil hadn't felt for a long time and it gave him a sense of cautious optimism.

Goddamn he feels good in my arms. Maybe this is what I've been waiting for?

"This is really nice," murmured Torquil. "I haven't done this for a while."

"Fucked all day?"

"No, well, it has been a little while for that too, but what I meant was I haven't been comfortable with someone like this, after the sex was done, in a long time. I haven't really wanted it, to be honest."

Stop it! You're going to scare him away. Shut up, shut up, shut up!

Turning his head, Joao gave Torquil a mischievous grin with an equally roguish glint to his eyes.

"Oh, the sex isn't done, my handsome Scotsman. And you aren't getting rid of me that easily."

"Good to know." A warm glow flooded Torquil's chest. "I've really enjoyed my time with you."

"I am off tomorrow too, if you're up for it?"

"Yes, Sir."

The pair began to kiss under the moonlight in an increasingly amorous manner, and it appeared like they were headed into their umpteenth round for the day. Looking into Joao's eyes, Torquil's heart flickered with the start of something new.

Maybe Alisa was right, after all?

EDEN REVISITED

Steve Thomas never imagined that he'd end up in such a place; certainly not in this most unlikely of positions. It wasn't the room itself that was the problem, per se – actually it was quite a luxurious suite at the Grand Babylon Hotel. Rather, it was the fact that he was using said suite to dress himself in a moderately expensive black suit before heading off to get married… again.

Years ago, after his first marriage ended so badly, Steve fervently vowed that he wouldn't put himself, or anyone else, through such a horrific process again. To be perfectly honest, he'd known it was a huge mistake long before they'd even said 'I do', but he'd ignored his misgivings and plunged headlong into matrimony regardless. A main part of the reason he'd gone through with it was due to his foolish hope that marrying a woman would somehow cure his gayness – it didn't. If anything, being trapped in a sham of a marriage only served to increase his desire for masculine flesh. Not to say he didn't give it a darn good try, mind you. Sadly, despite the physical attractiveness of his wife, Melanie, with her flowing blonde locks, blue eyes, pretty button nose, pouty lips, and trim, Barbie-esque figure, it just wasn't what Steve craved. Their relationship had been tumultuous at best…toxic at worst.

Things had come to a crashing end about two years into their marriage when she'd caught Steve right in the middle of fucking their upstairs neighbor, Brian, over the large clothes dryer in the laundry room of their building. Steve had been so engrossed in his actions that he hadn't realized that Melanie was there until he felt boxes of laundry powder being hurled into his back. To be fair, the gent under him was fairly distracting – six feet of well-built manhood with an ass that could crack walnuts.

In addition to the detergent boxes there was much flinging of insults, delivered in an increasingly shrill tone.

"Fucking faggot! How could you do this to me! You disease-ridden piece of shit, I can't believe I ever let you touch me. You're disgusting! A fucking piece of filth!"

While Brian had yanked up his pants and skedaddled away at breakneck speed, Steve had simply stood there and silently taken everything that she dished out. The tirade had gone on for a good half hour.

I deserve it all. I'm worthless scum. I wish I was dead.

Unsurprisingly, a rather acrimonious divorce followed shortly thereafter. In order to be done with the whole mess,

Steve willingly gave her the apartment and the money in their savings account, leaving him only with his clothes and his beloved, if somewhat dilapidated, red Chevy. At the time, Steve believed he had nothing to lose. His reputation lay in tatters courtesy of his ex-wife, or more truthfully, he'd managed that himself by screwing Brian and she'd simply made sure that everyone knew about it. The shame he felt over his actions, and inability to control his homosexual impulses, ensured there were no heartfelt goodbyes with the few friends he'd accumulated during his time with Melanie.

Quitting his job, as the head zookeeper at the Starling City Zoo, Steve fled to start over somewhere new, leaving everyone he'd known behind him. He'd already built up a successful life from scratch once before so he knew he could do it again. After driving clear across the country, Steve found himself arriving in the bustling metropolis of Port Davinica. Wanting to make a complete break with his past, he took a job as a janitor at a rundown gym – although cleaning up after the gym beasts wasn't too far off his former profession.

As the months passed, he became restless with his new life. The sense of disgrace he'd felt faded and his naturally ambitious streak resurfaced, causing him to yearn for something more. To this end, he set his sights higher and convinced his employer to let him occasionally man the gym reception desk. From here, after a few years of hard work and with the aid of night courses, Steve became a successful personal trainer, transforming his already bulky frame into a mountain of muscle in the process.

Five years later, when the owners of the gym wanted to sell, Steve jumped at the opportunity. He recognized that the area was going through a renaissance, with the manicured hands of gentrification gradually transforming the formerly sketchy district into a popular destination – in particular with gay men. Capitalizing on this, along with some finance from the bank, Steve renovated and rebranded the ramshackle gym, upgrading the facilities and renaming it – Sweat Station. To ensure its success, Steve took a business course at the local community college, as well as doing a great deal of extracurricular research to help him avoid the pitfalls of being a new business owner. The hiring of handsome, strapping men for the reception area and the gym floor, also undoubtedly contributed to making it a thriving business.

Even with all his newfound success there was still the sense of something missing. Steve didn't want to admit it to himself, but he was lonely, which by way of a fairly long journey was how he ended up in the hotel room. Since arriving in Port Davinica, Steve hadn't forged any close friendships or even properly dated, unwilling to risk the pain of rejection. His brusque, closed-off attitude often came across as being aloof and a little mean-spirited, which served him well in the persona of a tough businessman but had left his personal life rather desolate.

Despite the strangeness of his current situation, Steve was feeling relatively calm. Admittedly, the circumstances of this marriage were vastly different than that of his previous one. For a start, he was marrying a man this time – he had come to terms with his sexuality a good decade or so beforehand. That being said, settling down with the man of his dreams still wasn't something he'd envisioned for his future. Of course, that was all before he'd met Adam Cartwright.

* * *

Looking for a life-long partner was the furthest thing from Steve's mind when Adam literally walked in through his front door – well, the entrance of the gym, at any rate.

It was just after five in the morning, on an already warm, late spring day, and Steve stood alone in the gym kitchen, making himself a protein smoothie. He preferred to exercise early in the day before the gym opened so that members wouldn't pester him during his workout. Clad in only a skimpy pair of red shorts, which were moist with exertion and clung to his sizeable package, Steve's hairy body was pumped-up in a most pleasing fashion. His exposed skin was taut over his bulging muscles and glistened with a light sheen of sweat.

Hearing the glass front door open, Steve turned towards the entrance and saw a tall, lean lad dressed in faded jeans and a loose fitting, sky-blue t-shirt, with shoulder length auburn hair and a smattering of freckles across the bridge of his nose. In his hands, he held two white rectangular boxes. He came past the reception desk and stopped short when he caught sight of Steve standing in the doorway to the kitchen.

"Excuse me, Si..Sir," said Adam, obviously flustered. "I'm Adam. I…I have a delivery of a…"

I do like being called, Sir. Why is he so nervous? I could certainly give him some stress relief. Stop it! He looks barely legal.

Steve had caught glimpses of the delivery boy before but hadn't really paid much attention, as Adam was hardly the type he went for, favoring more muscular guys around his own age. Besides he never wanted to be accused of robbing the cradle – nothing sadder than appearing to be chasing after one's lost youth, after all. That aside, there was something about the shy and stammering boy, which caused a familiar feeling in Steve's groin, as his manhood began to rouse in the confinement of his underwear. There was also a curious new sensation brewing inside Steve that couldn't quite identify.

What else would I want from him?

The lanky redhead was making a delivery of low-fat, high-protein muffins from the patisserie next door, Dom's Delights, to sell in the gym's café. Originally, Steve had been embroiled in a dispute with owner of the patisserie, as since it opened they'd been eating into his customer base, luring gym members away with their admittedly superior product.

The pair had consequently settled their differences with a furious bout of fucking in the back stairwell of the gym – a most effective method of mediation. Once spent, they'd both been calm enough to work out an understanding that benefitted them both. Today was the first day of this new arrangement.

"The muffins, yeah. You can put them in here." Steve moved back into the kitchen to give Adam room to pass. "On the counter by the sink."

"Um…sure, OK."

After a brief hesitation, Adam followed Steve's direction but when he came into the close quarters of the kitchen, his eyes seemed to be darting everywhere except for on Steve.

I think I know what his problem is.

Admiring the way the delivery boy's tight jeans cradled his perky little ass, Steve moved to the centre of the kitchen. After putting the boxes on the counter, Adam was in such a rush to leave he hadn't noticed that Steve had moved and so ran straight into the hard wall of muscle and nearly fell backwards.

Instinctively, Steve reached forward and caught him in a firm grasp. It felt good holding him, their bodies pressed tightly together, and Steve was in no rush to let go. He breathed in the aroma of the delivery boy, an alluring combination of perspiration and a citrus-scented deodorant. Adam's face was a maelstrom of emotion – fear and excitement the most prominent.

"I'm so, so sorry about that but I…"

Adam's apology was quickly hushed with a passionate kiss. Steve felt Adam relax into the embrace and a hardness poking into him from beneath the delivery boy's jeans.

Mmm…feels like a decent size package.

Normally, this is where Steve would have proceeded to have his wicked way with the lad right there on the kitchen floor – it certainly wouldn't be the first time he'd used the gym for his trysts. Adam, however, apparently had other ideas. Breaking free, Adam dashed out of the kitchen as fast as his lithe legs could carry him.

"See you tomorrow!" Steve called out to Adam's retreating form.

Intrigued, Steve chuckled to himself. The delivery boy was the first man to refuse him in a very long time.

So, he wants to play hard to get? I'll have him begging for it by the end of the week. Pity though, I could have done with a quickie.

Fortunately, Steve managed to obtain some much-needed relief later that day when he was called to deal with a report of inappropriate behavior in the steam room. Not that he minded what the guys got up to but sometimes a member would get put out by the shenanigans of others – especially if they weren't being included. Walking into the change room, Steve flung open the steam room door and found two fit-looking gents that he recognized as regulars, in the middle of a rather enthusiastic embrace. His first thought had been to stop them but his encounter with Adam had left him more than a little riled up. Grabbing both men roughly by the arms, Steve pulled them into the nearest toilet cubicle and thoroughly reprimanded them with his cock. Needless to say it wasn't much of a deterrent, but everyone got what he deserved.

Despite Steve's prediction of being able to easily bed the delivery boy it turned out to be a far more drawn out process. Over the next few weeks, Steve and Adam became involved in a fascinating game of cat and mouse. Neither of the pair ever mentioned the incident in the kitchen but an unmistakable tension underlay each of their exchanges. For his part, Adam had an aura of caution about him, dropping off the boxes and leaving with the barest of pleasantries. Steve, on the other hand, adopted the thoroughly unfamiliar role of the perfect gentleman. Unwilling to startle his prey a second time, he was content to bide his time. It had been a long time since he was challenged in such a manner. To his great surprise, Steve found a protective instinct rising in him, as opposed to feeling merely predatory towards the sweet-faced, yet thoroughly tempting, delivery boy.

Eventually, their interactions took on a friendlier tone and they began chatting to one another; at first just innocent comments about the weather but gradually building up to more personal subjects, such as plans for the weekend. This was completely new territory for Steve as he felt a strange desire to actually get to know this lad as opposed to the many men he'd simply treated as useful bits of meat.

As the weeks went by, Steve couldn't help but notice that Adam seemed to be developing more self-assurance. Gone was the guarded demeanor and in its place an almost cocky persona. The change intrigued Steve even more and he pondered what exactly he'd gotten himself into.

I still want to fuck him senseless…but maybe something a little more too? Ergh, I'm turning into a soppy pansy! I should just finish what I started that morning and move on. Get him onto my cock and then out of my system.

In an unexpected turn of events, Steve didn't get a chance to carry out his plan. The following morning Adam walked in, set down his boxes, marched straight up to Steve and kissed him in a most ardent fashion, before breaking away. Steve, while somewhat startled, promptly responded in kind, pushing him back up against the sink in the kitchen and eagerly violated the young mouth with his tongue in return. This continued for a few minutes before Adam forcefully pushed Steve back.

"If you want more you're going to have to take me out."

He's certainly grown some balls. I like it. Cocky little bastard.

"Do I just?" replied Steve in a slightly mocking tone.

"Fine then."

Turning on his heel, Adam went to stride out of the kitchen when Steve shot out his arm and dragged him back into a tight clinch. Adam struggled but Steve could tell that it was half-hearted at best.

"Not so fast." Steve kissed him forcefully and pulled him in even tighter. "Meet me here tonight at 7."

"Dinner and a movie?"

"Maybe."

Adam went to leave again, although Steve was even less convinced of his determination to actually exit the kitchen.

"OK then, Red. Whatever you want."

A wide smile broke across Adam's face and Steve felt a fluttering inside his chest in response.

What was that? I've never felt that before.

To shrug off the unexpected surge of emotion, Steve gave Adam one more vigorous kiss before releasing him back to the rest of his deliveries. The rest of his day passed by in a bit of a haze, as his mind kept drifting back to that kiss and the promise of what the night would bring. That's not to say there wasn't a trace of hesitation in his thoughts.

What did I agree to? I haven't been on a date since... Melanie. I don't even remember how to date. What's the worst that can happen? I could fuck it up and not get sex. What am I doing?

Steve's slight qualms proved completely unfounded. The date was a smashing success and they had barely finished their mains at the nearby Cantonese restaurant – Mr. Kong's – before Adam surprised Steve once again.

"How about we forget about the movie and just go back to yours for dessert?" Adam's lascivious tone left no room for misunderstanding.

Not needing any further encouragement, Steve paid the check and swiftly whisked Adam back home to fervently consummate a few months worth of mutual lust and longing.

Twenty minutes later, they were furiously making out in the hallway of Steve's apartment, urgently grasping at one another as their tongues sparred together. It seemed that they were going to fuck right there against the wall until Adam slowed things down to gently kissing. This was a new experience for Steve, as he wasn't used to softness in his sexual encounters. He had gone from teenage fumbles in locker rooms and cramped back seats into the more frenzied, fast sessions with anonymous guys in sauna cabins. He didn't know what it was about Adam that drew out this gentler side of him but he wasn't opposed to it…for the moment.

After a few minutes the tenderness gave way to unbridled passion. Clothes were quickly discarded and Steve easily hoisted Adam up so that his legs were wrapped around his waist and carried him into the bedroom. Throwing Adam down on the bed, Steve jumped on top of him, covering Adam's lean form with his own muscular build. They rolled around and explored each other's bodies, taking the time to discover all the sensitive spots and pleasure each other fully. Steve was soon a great fan of the delivery boy's smooth, lean body. He took much delight in finding and kissing all the little freckles spread about Adam's pale skin. Adam, in turn, happily played with Steve's body hair, running his fingers, then his tongue, all through the more hirsute areas, especially the armpits and ass crack. The latter soon had all of his attention as he thrust his face as deep inside Steve's thoroughly enticing entrance as humanly possible. Adam was far from the innocent that he appeared to be.

Normally, Steve wasn't that interested in being rimmed but Adam was doing such a spectacular job he felt no desire to stop him feasting on his ass. Steve was very much impressed with Adam's skill and even found himself pushing back against the apparently very ravenous mouth.

From here they happily and hungrily moved on to each other's cocks, giving each of them just as much eager attention. Steve was happy to see that Adam's manhood was almost as long as his own eight inches, if somewhat thicker. Their sweaty bodies stayed tightly wrapped up together, as their movements varied between fierce and frenzied through to gentle and loving. At this point, Steve would have usually taken control and just plowed Adam's hot, white ass without a second thought, but the whole encounter had thrown him out of his comfort zone and had him keen to try something new. So, in a move that was completely out of character, Steve made an offer that was a bit of a shock to even himself.

"Wanna fuck me?"

Indeed, everyone – Steve included - would have said the possibility of Britney singing live was a far more likely option than his ever willingly taking on a passive role.

"Really? I just assumed that you'd want to top me."

"I fully intend on doing that later but if you don't want it, then I can just…"

"On your back," commanded Adam. "Spread your legs."

Damn, that's hot.

"You'll have to go slow," instructed Steve. "It's… ah…been a long time."

Not that this was a kindness Steve had shown to the many others who'd asked the same of him, mind you. Granted, Steve's conquests tended not to complain once the pain of the rough fucking had faded into far more pleasant sensations. Steve was far less experienced than he'd ever admit to. Truth be told, the only action his ass had seen in the last few years was the occasional dildo after a drunken night out when he needed to scratch a certain itch. It wasn't that he was against being fucked; it was more that he didn't like the loss of control.

Why am I so comfortable with him?

"Don't worry, Grizzly," reassured Adam, in response to the show of unexpected vulnerability. "I'll treat you right."

Steve generously applied lube to himself and Adam's condom-covered cock and nervously waited for Adam to penetrate him. Adam took his position at the entrance, supporting Steve's thick, muscular legs up against his body. They locked eyes as Adam slowly pushed himself inside Steve's hairy hole.

Gritting his teeth at the initial pain of penetration, Steve clamped his ass muscles down on the invading inches. Forcing himself to relax, he felt Adam pushing in deeper with each stroke and was soon raising his hips up to meet him. Although Adam had started softly, Steve's groans of enjoyment soon had him furiously pounding away. Steve loved the feel of Adam driving his manhood into his virgin-like ass. Neither of them lasted particularly long, the extended courtship having taken its toll. Mere moments after Steve's load exploded out of his member and coated his chest in thick, white cream; Adam reached his own release ably filling the protective sheath with his seed.

Adam collapsed down onto Steve's burly chest, leaving his still erect member lodged deep inside the warm passage. There were many rounds that night, with much flip-flopping – versatility being a much-valued virtue – until both were rather sore but smilingly sated. Their fucking was more intense than Steve thought he'd wanted, although this was hardly surprising given how smitten he'd quickly become with the boy.

Skipping the second date altogether, the gents found themselves in a relationship, spending a great deal of their free time buggering each other silly. Of course, when news got out of their involvement the new couple was subject to the occasional biblical joke about snakes and eating each other's forbidden fruit but it was all in good humor.

Their inability to keep their hands to themselves, as is the case with most new entanglements, meant that Adam's morning deliveries had started taking longer and longer with his spending an inordinate amount of time in the gym kitchen.

Quality customer service.

* * *

The relationship soon began to change Steve in ways that he'd never expected. Whether it was Adam's bright-eyed optimism or his free and open manner, he couldn't be sure, but the delivery boy had managed to pierce the gruff, frosty exterior that Steve had cultivated over the years. At first, Steve had been a little scared to be putting himself out there, afraid of rejection and being hurt, but as the weeks turned into months, he felt the tension easing and began to relax into this new, more open version of himself. Little-by-little, Steve became friendlier to those around him with many staff members and gym-goers noticing the change for the better. While he still projected an air of dominance it was now tinged with an ingenuousness that made him far more approachable.

In the past, he'd had a hard time opening up to people given his family history. He didn't like to talk about it, as he wanted to forget it even happened. Often Steve changed the subject whenever the topic of family arose but Adam hadn't been deterred and had gently coaxed the not particularly heartwarming story out of him.

My life story isn't that great. I don't want people to think of me as a victim…especially Adam.

Steve's upbringing had hardly been idyllic and even though his parents were now long dead, the pain he'd endured was still very much alive. He'd left home at the tender age of fifteen, unable to take the emotional and physical abuse any longer. His father had been a violent drunk, who'd left his shares of bruises and psychological marks. There'd been several visits to the hospital over his childhood, the most severe being for the treatment of a broken wrist – the result of a five-year-old Steve watching television too loudly the morning after one of his father's benders. Social services had visited the house on several occasions, but his parents terrorized Steve into keeping quiet, making him genuinely believe that the foster system was a worse alternative to what he already had.

His mother was a weak-willed woman and a borderline alcoholic herself, who offered next to no protection for her two defenseless children. Steve's older sister, Emily, fled the family home five years before he'd made his own escape. The siblings had only had sporadic contact ever since.

The day he'd finally had enough came just a few days after his fifteenth birthday. Steve had come from school to find his father drunkenly-dozing on the sofa surrounded by empty beer cans. On the television, there was a repeat of an old football game, the sound blaring.

He's such a fucking cliché.

Moving to the television, Steve switched it off and went to go to his bedroom. Before he could leave, his awakening father waylaid him.

"What do you think you're doing?" slurred his father. "I was watching that, faggot."

Even though it was a familiar slur, a chill went through Steve. Not accepting of his own sexuality, he could only imagine what punishment his father would met out of he ever learnt of Steve's secret yearnings.

"You were asleep."

Jumping to his feet surprisingly quickly given his level of intoxication, his father pushed Steve violently backwards against the armchair in the corner.

"Don't fucking talk back to me, boy!"

The years of resentment and anger came boiling to the surface and in a blind, white-hot rage Steve got to his feet and slammed his fist into father's face as hard as he could. There was an awful cracking sound as his fist connected and sent his father falling hard to the floor, where he stayed. Steve stood there motionless for several agonizing seconds, watching the slow rise and fall of his father's chest.

"Dad?"

Nothing but light breathing greeted his inquiry.

It was then that his mother entered the room looking somewhat bewildered, obviously several drinks into her day. She paused by the sofa, slowly taking in the scene before her.

"Al?" she called to her husband in a panic. "Al, what's happened?"

Steve's mother stumbled forward to her husband and saw the rapidly developing bruise on the left side of his face and evidently connected the dots.

"What have you done to him?" she screeched. "He's your father!"

"He started it!" growled Steve defensively.

"You ungrateful little brat! After all we've done for you."

She lunged forward, arms flailing but in her drunken state Steve was easily able to knock her harmlessly back onto the sofa and turned away from the pitiful scene.

"Don't you dare walk away from me," threatened his mother. "Get back here, Steve!"

Knowing that he would face a terrible retribution if he stayed, Steve rushed to his room, packed a rucksack full of clothes and left the house while his mother continued to scream obscenities.

Fortunately, he had a few friends to crash with over the following weeks but he'd soon left school to find menial work in order to support himself. After a month or so of working two jobs – McDonalds during the day and a pizzeria in the evening – he was able to scrape and save and get a tiny place of his own. It was a dive, with dodgy plumbing and a roach problem but at least he was no longer in danger of daily beatings.

After a few years of work at the pizzeria, he was promoted to day manager and was able to attend night classes to obtain his high school diploma. From here, he managed to get an internship at the zoo to pursue his interest in animals. He'd always been fascinated by the animal kingdom and was disappointed as child when his requests for pets were always rejected. Looking back, it was probably for the best given his parents lack of regard for other living creatures.

After that fateful afternoon, Steve had no further contact with his parents. It was only through hearing a news report on his car radio, on the way to work one morning, where he heard their names given as the sole fatalities in a car accident – his father was drunk behind the wheel.

At least they didn't take anyone else with them. Good riddance.

He never shed a tear for them and it had stayed that way. He'd never even told Melanie about them, only saying that his parents had died when he was young. It was a story he never thought he'd relive but that was before Adam came into his life.

They were lying in bed one Sunday morning after yet another fervent bout of fucking when Steve finally told Adam the entire story, including his disastrous marriage to Melanie. It felt good to finally speak about his upbringing, his heart seeming lighter than it had for a very long time. The redhead was silent the entire time, a serious regard upon his face.

When Steve finished, he looked towards Adam, half-afraid of what he may say.

Will that scare him off? It's a lot to take in. I'm damaged goods.

"Thank you for telling me," said Adam as he took Steve's hand in his. "I'm so sorry that happened to you."

"I don't need your pity," responded Steve gruffly, his defenses raised.

"No, of course not. I just think it sucks but I'm also fucking amazed that you managed to pull your life together after all that."

"I guess."

"You guess?" asked Adam, his voice full of disbelief. "You're a legend in my books, Mister."

"Really?"

In response, Adam leaned up and brushed his lips gently against Steve's.

"Really."

With a cheeky grin, Adam began to kiss his way down Steve's increasingly excited body. The past out in the open, Steve dived enthusiastically into his present, spending the rest of the day pleasuring his boyfriend in all manner of delightfully debauched ways.

* * *

About six months after they'd started dating, Steve was faced with a rather daunting proposition.

"I want you to meet my parents," stated Adam, out-of-the-blue one morning at breakfast, after staying the night at Steve's.

"You what?" asked Steve, nearly choking on his muesli.

"Meet my parents. I mean we've been dating a while and I wanted them to get to know you."

"Yeah, I'm sure they'll be thrilled that an old guy like me is defiling their child."

"Ha! I was corrupted a long time before you came along," joked Adam. "Besides, my dad is at least *five* years older than you."

"That's not comforting," grumbled Steve. "Do I have to meet them so soon?"

"Yes, you do and it'll be fine. They've met boyfriends before...although you are definitely the oldest," needled Adam with a malicious glee.

"Keep that up and this *old man* will show you exactly how much life he has left in him."

"Promises, promises."

Adam's half-mocking tone stirred up Steve's inner beast – not that he was ever too far from the surface. Throwing back his chair, Steve lunged forward and effortlessly hoisted Adam over his shoulder before he even had time to protest.

He carried his squirming boyfriend down the hall and proceeded to do all manner of things that showcased just how much stamina he had in reserve. When they were done and laying a most pleasant post-coital afterglow and shiny with sweat, Adam recommenced his attack.

"So, about that dinner…"

"I've already met your brother and your sister, isn't that enough?"

"Nope. I want to show off *my man* to all my family!"

He's not going to let this go. I might as well get it over and done with.

"Fine. Next week then?"

"Great! I'll set it up." Adam gave Steve a loving peck on the lips and settled back into his boyfriend's arms. "They'll be thrilled to meet you!"

We'll see about that.

Steve's objections to meeting Adam's parents weren't completely related to their fifteen-year age difference. It was a big step in their relationship and hinted towards a future that Steve had long ago dismissed as being for him. Besides, the last set of parents he'd met were Melanie's and they hadn't been exactly impressed with him.

As it turned out, Steve was more than a little thrown by the way Adam's parents reacted to meeting their son's older man. From the moment that they walked in the door, Steve was greeted with open arms.

"Steve, it's so lovely to meet you," exclaimed Adam's mother, Melissa, giving Steve a kiss on the cheek. "Adam has told us so much about you."

She was a full-figured woman, in her early fifties, with green eyes and cropped auburn hair the same shade as her son's. Her husband, Frank, was a tall, portly, bearded gent with short blond hair and hazel eyes. Together, they made for a pleasing couple.

"Yes, it's good to meet the man that's making my boy so happy," added Frank, grasping Steve's hand in a very firm shake. "Even if you are a bit long in the tooth."

I knew they'd be unhappy about it!

"Dad!" scolded Adam, shooting father a look of exasperation.

"I'm joking, I'm joking." Frank grinned. "I'm sure Steve knows that. Don't you, Steve?"

"Well, I…"

"Good, good! Let's move into the living room for an aperitif, shall we?"

The foursome continued and had a most agreeable evening together. The tenseness that had Steve wound up tightly since their arrival slowly began to release and by the main course – a succulent roast chicken and baked vegetables – he'd actually begun to enjoy himself.

This isn't half bad at all.

"It must be good to own a gym. Easy to work out I imagine," pondered Melissa. "Lord knows I need to."

"You're perfect as is," countered Frank.

Steve felt a small grin come to his lips as he took in the loving domesticity. Glancing over at Adam, he saw his boyfriend looking at him with an adoring gaze.

How did I get so lucky to deserve him?

They parted on friendly terms with Melissa insisting on seeing them again very soon for dinner. Later that evening, when Steve was in bed with his arms wrapped around Adam, his thoughts were a little maudlin but edged with optimism.

I thought families like that only existed on TV. It felt nice to be part of that…to belong. Why couldn't I have had that growing up? Maybe, I can still have it…with Adam.

* * *

Several weeks after the parental dinner, the pair came to yet another important juncture in their coupledom. Since they'd gotten together, Adam began to spend more and more time at Steve's apartment, in fact they were living together for all intents and purposes. Adam had left a growing collection of clothes and toiletries to the point where Steve had had to clear a few drawers out to make space. It was Adam, once again, who pushed things along when he came to Steve with a request.

"So, I need another drawer."

"Another one?" exclaimed Steve, only half-serious. "At this rate you're practically moved in."

"Why don't I?"

He wants to what?

"Ummm…I wasn't…"

"Yeah, I know you were kidding, but why not? I have so much stuff here already. I sleep here most nights. We don't tend to annoy one another too much domestically…well apart from your inability to use a dishwasher properly."

"I have my own system."

"If you say so," scoffed Adam. "Anyway, if I can get past that then I'm sure we won't kill each other. So what do you say?"

Are we ready for that? Am I ready for that? What if it all falls apart? But what if it doesn't. Maybe I should be more like Adam and just go with it?

Truthfully, it had been something Steve had already considered but more in a fanciful kind of a way than an actual possibility. Throwing caution to the wind, Steve decided to take a leap of faith. Although, there was one nagging doubt he needed to clear up before they could proceed.

"If we're properly living together does that mean you want to be monogamous?" asked Steve, not exactly sure which answer he actually wanted to hear.

Even though they were only dating one another exclusively, the pair had granted their sexual encounters more flexibility…happily keen for a threesome…or foursome…or moresome. Originally, it was more at Steve's insistence, partly because he wasn't ready to open himself up completely and he didn't want to tie Adam down too early in his life. To be honest, Steve got off on watching Adam fucking and being fucked by other guys, especially big musclemen from the gym. Another semi-regular addition to their bed was Adam's best friend, Sebastian – a well-hung lad had longish, surfer blond locks, startling blue eyes and a tanned swimmer's physique...always a guaranteed good time. Not to say, that they hadn't gone on their separate play-dates on occasion when the other hadn't been available. That aside, of late, Steve found himself preferring to simply pleasure himself until Adam was available...although he wasn't about to forsake all others just yet.

"God, no! I mean, maybe one day." Adam hastily continued after apparently realizing how harsh he sounded. "I love you and *adore* our sex but I really like how we have things...open."

"Yeah, I do too. I just wasn't sure where we were headed."

"For now, I'm happy to leave things as is, after I officially move in. We've got time to figure it out, you aren't getting rid of me yet, Grizzly."

So, at the end of the month, Adam officially moved in and to Steve's great relief nothing really changed.

What was I so scared of?

* * *

Sadly, as much as it seemed like a fairytale romance, problems began to arise in their Eden. They'd been dating for around two years at this point and their lives were in a bit a state of flux. For his part, Steve was in the middle of a major remodel of the gym – completely redoing the change rooms and reception area, as well as transforming the rooftop into a relaxation area for the members. It was well overdue and the recent opening of another men-only gym two blocks away had put a dent in business, so Steve was doing his level best to woo his clients back. As with most renovation work there had been several delays and disgruntled customers unhappy with any interruption to their schedules – Steve was beginning to think he could have rebuilt the entire gym by himself in the same amount of time.

For his part, Adam was busy balancing his delivery job, his marketing studies and all the work required to help establish a new business. Adam, along with his friend, Daniel Applewhite – a handsome Englishman and tailor of some note – were launching a new brand of underwear – CocKed. It was obviously targeted to gentlemen of a certain persuasion.

Their increasingly busy schedules meant that they'd been spending less and less time together, which understandably affected their relationship. It was small things at first, bickering over seemingly inconsequential matters, such as who'd left the milk out of the refrigerator that morning but their arguments became more frequent and more public. It soon become glaringly obvious to those closest to Adam and Steve that they were going through something of a rough patch – and it wasn't just their penchant for handcuffs.

Steve was at a bit of a loss. His limited experience with relationships hadn't really prepared him on how to handle conflict. Usually, whenever things got difficult emotionally he'd moved on.

I don't want to lose him.

One Wednesday night, after another such fight, things came to a head.

"We can't go on like this, Grizzly," lamented Adam. "It's exhausting."

"I know. I hate fighting with you but we just always seem to be annoying the fuck out of each other."

"Look, I don't think it's either of our faults really, but we need to figure it out...and I think that I have a solution. We should make some time to get away from everything that's going on for a few days, so we can really talk things out. There's a cabin up in Christie National Park we could stay at and just be by ourselves. Actually, to be honest, it was Sebastian's idea, his cousin owns the cabin."

He's been sharing our personal stuff?

"You've been talking to all your friends about our problems?" questioned Steve in a harsher tone than he'd meant.

"Well it's hardly like it's a secret that we've been fighting."

"Yes, but I don't like everyone knowing my business."

"It's not everyone," refuted Adam defensively. "It was only Daniel and Sebastian."

"I don't care. You know how I value my privacy."

"I don't want to fight anymore. I'm sorry if you feel like I broke your trust but I love you and I want to fix what's wrong between us. Please, will you think about it?"

Hearing the desperation in Adam's voice, coupled with the pleading look in his eyes, was enough to soften Steve's stance. He forced to himself to calm down again and do what was best for his relationship.

"OK," agreed Steve with a resigned air.

"OK, you'll think about it or OK you want to do it?"

"We should do it…It's a good idea…no matter who came up with it."

It took a little bit of doing but the lads were able to organize time away for themselves in two weekends time. Daniel eagerly offered to handle all of the underwear business in Adam's absence and Steve's assistant manager, Gabriel, was more than happy to oversee the renovations. He was a capable lad, with cropped bleach blond hair, dark inviting eyes, smooth ebony skin and a body that proclaimed his love of exercise.

"Yeah, we've all noticed that you've been a bit more of a bear than usual," commented Gabriel, after Steve had briefly explained the reason for his impromptu trip.

"Hey, watch it," threatened Steve light-heartedly. "I'm still your boss."

"Only until we rise up and mutiny."

Two years ago, that remark, no matter how tongue-in-cheek, would have drawn Steve's ire – not that anyone would've been game enough to make such a remark. Now he was able to take it all in his stride.

Adam really is a good influence on me.

"Cheeky bugger. Just make sure the gym doesn't fall down while I'm away."

"We'll try, my liege."

The last remark was a touch too far and Steve smacked Gabriel on the ass with a resounding whack for his insolence – not that Gabriel appeared to mind in the slightest.

And so, with their lives on hold and time on their hands, the duo packed their car and set off for their getaway. The journey took a few hours, and the last few miles seemed to take forever as it meant driving along a narrow, winding dirt road, but the chance offered by this trip was well worth it. The cabin itself was rather rustic but contained all the essentials for a relaxing retreat…including a large and extremely comfy bed. It was situated fairly high up in the mountains and had stunning views back down the valley and westward to the ocean. The woods surrounding the cabin were quite thick but there were a few trails where one could hike and commune with nature. The couple soon found that the crisp mountain air made a refreshing change from the city pollution.

Within five minutes of arriving, they discovered that there was no television, no Internet and limited phone reception – nothing to interrupt their reconciliation. It wasn't easy at first, as the problems had been building up for a while and Steve had never been one to be particularly open about his feelings. It took a day or so but eventually they began to talk more openly and honestly than they ever had before. Their discussions revealed deeper issues, such as Steve's insecurity at being older than Adam – only fifteen years but an eon to some – and the accompanying fear that Adam would leave him for someone younger.

"You're not too old for me." Adam gently reassured his boyfriend. "…but there's something I need to tell you."

Adam appeared reluctant to continue, so Steve moved forward and gave him a heartening hug.

"You know you can tell me anything."

"OK, I don't want you to freak out but I need to honest with you." Adam plowed on, knowing that he needed to get it out. "I'm…I *was* starting to have feelings for someone else…for Connor."

"Connor? Your web designer?"

Adam nodded and Steve was at a loss. He felt a little light-headed, as his stomach knotted and tears pricked at the corner of his eyes. Steve's emotions were in a tailspin.

I knew it! Maybe this is karma for what happened with Melanie. Why wouldn't he want someone younger instead of a dinosaur like me?

"Do you want to leave me for him?" asked Steve, when he'd recovered enough to speak.

"No! Of course, not. I love you. My feelings towards you haven't changed and I'm prepared to do whatever it takes to get our relationship back on track."

Relief flooded through Steve and he couldn't help but give a little smile, bolstered by the news that all was not lost. They continued to talk, with the occasional tears flowing on both sides, as the tension between them slowly began to dissipate.

To help improve their stressed relationship, they decided upon some new ground rules. Generously, Steve didn't demand that Adam cut all ties with Connor, as much as he may have wanted to, but he did insist that the sexual part of their relationship had to end. In that vein, they agreed to try monogamy for a while, so that they could focus all of their emotional and sexual energy in the place where it was most needed.

As the days went by the dark cloud hanging over them began to lift and it felt as if the spark was well and truly back. Once their issues were well on the way to being resolved, they spent the rest of the time fucking like honeymooners…all over the cabin and even managing to startle the local wildlife when the mood had taken them whilst hiking on more than one occasion.

"I love you, Grizzly," Adam murmured after one such saucy session.

"I love you, too, Red," replied Steve, brushing a long, red lock of Adam's hair aside and giving his boyfriend a playful kiss on his freckled nose.

They returned to Port Davinica feeling refreshed, and a little bit sore, but with a renewed commitment to one another to work harder at their relationship and not take each other for granted.

* * *

It was whilst lying in bed on a rainy Saturday morning, about a month after their trip, that Steve came to a decision, which would change his life completely. Gazing down at the slumbering form of his boyfriend, Steve's heart was full of emotion and he saw clearly where his future lay.

He's the best thing that's ever happened to me. I want to be with him forever.

Steve started plotting the proposal straight away, debating with himself for a few weeks over the perfect way to pop the question. He wanted it to be more than the clichéd going down on bended knee at a fancy restaurant, as was the case when he'd asked Melanie.

Look how that turned out! Besides, there are far better things to do on your knees.

Churning the idea over and over in his head, Steve searched for something unique but not overly sappy – he wasn't that changed a man, after all. Funnily enough, it was while he was at the gym, absentmindedly gazing at the posters advertising CocKed underwear, on the wall to the side of the cardio area, that the perfect solution came to him.

That would be awesome…if I can organize it. I can't do it alone.

Overcoming his aversion for asking for help, Steve turned to Adam's business partner to make the idea into a reality.

"I think it would be rather smashing," exclaimed Daniel, after Steve explained what he'd envisioned. "And I definitely think the fellows will be champing at the bit to be a part of it."

"Thanks," said Steve, his body physically relaxing as his plan began to come together. "You don't know how much I appreciate this."

"I have an idea," remarked Daniel, a knowing smile gracing his lips. "He's exceedingly important to me too."

And so, one week later, the day for the grand question had arrived.

Steve invited Adam to meet him up on the renovated roof of the gym, just as the sun was beginning to set. He'd closed the area to members around lunchtime and then moved the sun lounges, tables and chairs off to the edges. In the middle of the wooded platform, Steve had set up a picnic blanket with a hamper full of goodies and a bottle of champagne chilling to the side.

God, I hope he likes it.

After making sure that everything was ready, Steve nervously paced up and down until he heard the metallic click of the rooftop door opening. He greeted Adam with an enthusiastic kiss.

"Hey, you." Noticing the champagne, Adam gave Steve a quizzical look. "Special occasion?"

"Maybe. You never know," replied Steve being deliberately cryptic.

"Did I forget an anniversary?"

"Doubt it. You're always better at remembering that stuff than me."

"Can we sit down and eat? I'm starving!"

Adam went to move towards the picnic basket but Steve caught him by the arm.

"Before we eat, I wanna show you…something."

"What is it?"

"Just come over by the railing and you'll see."

As casually as he could muster, Steve walked over and leant against the metal railing.

"You aren't going to push me over, are you? I told you I was sorry about breaking that plate," joked Adam, poking his tongue out.

"Of course not!" Steve's tone was full of mock-exasperation. "Just get over here, silly boy."

Meandering over, Adam stood next to Steve and looked down.

"What the…?"

Down in the courtyard below were the CocKed models, in just their underwear, laying on the ground, each with a letter painted on them in fluorescent paint that was easily visible in the twilight. Together the bodies spelled out that very important question – Will You Marry Me?

Adam was stunned, his eyes watering he slowly turned towards Steve.

"You did all this for me?"

"Yes, I did. So?" asked Steve, hoping that he didn't sound too desperate.

"So, what?"

Steve grunted in frustration.

"Will you marry me?"

A sly grin spread over Adam's face, obviously enjoying teasing Steve.

"Of course, I will, Grizzly."

They embraced and kissed joyfully, bordering on indecently, to the cheers and the howls of the models below. A few minutes later, the lads were disrupted in their clinch by the arrival of aforementioned models with Daniel in tow. They were many, many cries of congratulations and flurries of kisses and hugs.

The revelry lasted quite a while with many a bottle of champagne – courtesy of Daniel – emptied in celebration. Eventually, the models and Daniel departed leaving the newly engaged couple together on the roof, sprawled together on the picnic blanket looking up at the stars.

"You've made me so happy," murmured Steve as he kissed the top of Adam's head.

"Right back at ya!"

Adam turned his face to meet Steve's and moved in for a kiss that lingered and inspired other body parts to join in on the action. Under the heavenly blanket, they made slow love to consummate their engagement.

This is the life.

* * *

Even though Steve's life was fuller than he ever thought possible, there was still a little something that niggled at him.

Throughout the wedding preparations, Steve saw how Adam got along with his parents and siblings and it stirred at long-repressed emotions.

I wish I could have had that.

The discomfort hadn't gone unnoticed by his fiancé, who brought it up after they'd returned home after meeting with the celebrant.

"So, are you going to tell me what's bothering you?" demanded Adam.

"No…it's nothing…everything it's fine."

"Bullshit."

"What?"

"You heard me. I know you well enough to know when something's wrong. We promised that we'd never keep anything from each other again. Tell me what's eating at you, please."

I guess I have to. Why does he have to be so damn perceptive?

"It's just that I see how close you are with your brother and your sister and…it made me think about Emily."

Sitting on the sofa next to his fiancé, Adam put his hand on Steve's leg and gave it a reassuring squeeze.

"Have you thought about trying to reconnect with her?"

"Yes and no, but I don't know if it'd be a good idea or not," admitted Steve. "We haven't spoken in years and I wouldn't even know how to find her."

"There are people for that. If you seriously want to get back in touch with her what better time is there than now? Isn't it time to bury the past?"

"Maybe…I guess."

"I'll support you no matter you decide."

"I appreciate that."

He's such a good man.

Due to Adam's encouragement, Steve decided to take the plunge and make peace with his past. To that end, he hired a private detective, Ruby Washington – a striking redhead with intelligent blue eyes and curves that she often used to her advantage.

"I'll be honest, there's not a lot to go on, Mr. Thomas, but I'll do my best to find her," stated Ruby, at the end of their first meeting.

I hope I'm doing the right thing. What if she wants nothing to do with me? Better to know and put everything behind me.

In a spot of good fortune, Emily proved not too difficult to find and Ruby brought happy news back to her client a mere two weeks later.

"I managed to track her down through court records. Your sister is married and now goes by the name Emily Rogers. She lives with her husband and two daughters in a small town a few hours drive from here called Magnolia Falls. Here are her contact details."

I can't believe it!

"Thanks, I appreciate your hard work."

"It was nothing," replied Ruby nonchalantly. "Don't forget to recommend me to your friends."

After deliberating for a few days, Steve worked up the courage to call her.

"Emily Rogers speaking, how may I help you?"

"Em…Emily, it's Steve…your brother."

There was a long pause and Steve immediately berated himself, fearing the worst.

Dammit! I should've left things alone. She has her own family now. She probably doesn't want me to mess up her new life.

"Stevie?" asked Emily sounding dazed. "Is it really you?"

"Yeah, it's me, Ememmy." The half-forgotten childhood nickname came unbidden to his lips.

"Oh my god! I can't believe it's you! I've tried looking for you a few times over the years but you disappeared without a trace."

"I know." Sadness and regret hung heavy in Steve's voice. "I'm sorry."

Before he could start feeling too sorry for himself, Steve was hit by a barrage of questions.

"How did you find me? Are you doing well? Where on Earth are you living? Are you married?"

"Hey, hold on there. Give me time to answer."

"Oh, Stevie. I'm sorry but I'm just so excited to hear from you. I never thought I would."

"I hired a detective and she told me where you were. I'm doing well and living in Port Davinica."

"Really? That's not far at all. Can you come up and see us? You can stay for the weekend. Your nieces would love to meet their Uncle Steve."

Uncle Steve? That sounds so weird.

"Umm, yeah. Sure, that would be great." Steve paused, unsure of how to broach the next subject. Finally, he decided that honesty was the best course. "Do you mind if I bring my fiancé Adam along?"

"Of course, not," replied Emily without missing a beat or seeming to lose any enthusiasm whatsoever. "We'd love to meet him too."

Letting out a sigh of relief, Steve could feel a broad grin stretching his face as he made plans for visiting his long-lost sister the following weekend.

The rest of the week flew by and after a tense, yet hopeful car ride, Steve stood before the front door of a charming weatherboard home, complete with white picket fence and well-maintained garden.

I guess she found her happy family dream too.

Summoning his courage again, Steve pressed the silver button of the doorbell and launched a pleasant jingle into the air.

"Stevie!" cried Emily, as she opened the door to her brother and Adam.

She appeared a good deal older than Steve remembered; it had been well over a decade since their last encounter, after all. Even so, she was still unmistakably his sister with her midnight black hair, and dark brown eyes that they shared. Despite having two kids she'd also kept her svelte figure.

Moving forward, Emily latched onto her little brother and gave him a fierce hug that seemed incongruous with her small frame. They held the embrace for a rather long time and soon tears were running from both their eyes.

"Oh dear, my make up is going to be ruined," lamented Emily, light-heartedly. "Come inside, before the neighbors think I've gone crazy."

They trooped inside to a round of introductions as Emily brought the two parts of her family together for the first time. After some initial awkwardness, they fell into conversation and were all chatting around the outdoor table on the back patio, while Emily's husband, Trevor – a hearty-looking man with friendly features – barbequed their lunch.

Later, after Steve's adorable nieces, Charlotte and Sophia, had gone to bed, Adam and Trevor had thoughtfully wandered off to allow the siblings some time to talk by themselves.

"I'm so sorry for leaving you there, Stevie," apologized Emily, her voice wavering slightly. "I could barely look after myself let alone you."

"I understand. It wasn't your fault or mine, it was *theirs*." The bitterness of Steve's tone was unmistakable. "I never blamed you. You *never* have to apologize to me."

"Thank you for that," murmured Emily, as she wiped the wetness from under her eyes. "I can't tell you how much that means to me."

"You seem to have built a good life. A lot better than what we had. You seem happy."

"I really am. Trevor has been amazing and so understanding about everything. It took a while but I finally got to a place where I could move past what happened and create a new life for myself. It hasn't all been sunshine and puppies but I do love it. And you? Are you happy?"

"Yeah…it's taken forever too. I never thought that I could be but Adam changed that for me."

"He certainly seems like a keeper…if slightly young. Not that I'm judging…much."

"Hey!" Enjoying the moment they were sharing, Steve decided to make a grand gesture. "So, we were wondering if you…and your family, would like to come to our wedding."

"Of course, Stevie. We'd be honored." Emily beamed. "I was hoping you'd ask but I didn't want to presume that you would. We wouldn't miss it for the world."

"That makes me really happy to hear you say that."

They continued chatting well into the early hours, after which Steve fell into bed, cuddled up with Adam, perhaps the happiest he'd ever been.

"Thank you for pushing me," whispered Steve. "I owe you so much."

"Any time, Grizzly."

The rest of the weekend passed far too quickly but was wrapped up in contented family bonding, with the sibling relationship well and truly rekindled. From here, the siblings remained in close contact, talking on the phone every few days and messaging on social media in the lead up to the wedding.

Feels good to have family again. I should have done this years ago. But would I have been ready before meeting Adam?

* * *

A sudden knock at the door disturbed his reminiscing. Checking his watch, Steve saw that it was almost time to go.

Here goes nothing.

Opening the door, Steve was treated to the pleasing sight of a rather dapper-looking Adam in a smart, bespoke navy blue suit that complemented Steve's own – it helped to have a tailor for a business partner.

"Ready to do this?" asked Adam, his face full of expectation.

"You betcha!"

Steve pulled Adam into a hungry kiss that helped steady his nerves. Predictably, the amorous embrace soon produced growing bulges in their suit pants, as they rubbed together.

"We shouldn't…" protested Adam feebly. "We'll be late."

"Come on just a quick one," begged Steve. "Let them wait."

Not to be deterred, Steve played unfairly and bit the sensitive spot on his husband-to-be's neck causing Adam to groan his appreciation.

"Bastard!"

They continued on in their manly sport for another few minutes, their clothing rapidly coming undone and hair beginning to become mussed.

"OK, that's enough," declared Adam as he pushed Steve away. "You'll have to make an honest man of me to get the rest."

Reluctantly acquiescing, Steve moved away and the lads began to make themselves presentable again.

"Fine, but your ass is mine tonight, Mister."

"Damn straight it is," agreed Adam with a cheeky grin. "Right after I have yours. Now let's get a move on."

After checking their reflections, to ensure they were once more presentable, the pair headed downstairs and outside to the front of the hotel. There, they hopped into the limousine that was waiting to ferry them up to the nearby bluffs, where their cliff-top wedding was scheduled to take place.

Fortunately, the day had dawned bright and clear and was expected to stay that way with nary a cloud marring the perfectly blue sky. Atop the bluff, there were several rows of blue chairs with white ribbons fluttering in the gentle ocean breeze. In front of these a small white wooden arch had been constructed where the celebrant, Margaret, a pleasantly plump lady in her mid-forties with frizzy brown hair and sparkling blue eyes, was waiting for them.

Steve's heart hammered in his chest as he took his place at the altar, and quickly looked out at all the expectant, smiling faces of their family and friends. His eyes caught

Emily's who was proudly sitting in the front row beside her husband and daughters. She gave him a reassuring smile and Steve found his nerves slowly beginning to subside.

This is all because of him. I'm a lucky man.

Standing across from Adam, Steve didn't think it was possible to be so happy and could barely resist to the urge to weep with joy; only the fact that it would ruin his uber-manly image held him in check.

As Adam began his vows, Steve felt a huge grin upon his face and tears pricking at his eyes.

I will not cry. I will not cry. I will not cry. Dammit, I'm crying!

Happily, his tears were more of a trickle than a full gushing fountain, so his mortification wasn't too severe. Taking a moment to compose himself, Steve took a deep breath before launching into his own vows. His deep, gravelly voice wavered slightly with the emotion of the day.

"Adam, before I met you I never thought that I was capable of love and definitely didn't think I deserved it. I still don't know what I did so right to have you come into my life but you've made me a better man. You've opened my eyes and my heart and I will spend the rest of my life showing just how much you mean to me. You are my love, my light, my everything."

The highly emotional words surprised many of the guests, who were used to the seeing Steve as a stoic, yet kind-hearted, man. To be honest, it continued to amaze Steve himself that he'd been able to speak so openly from his heart.

It was not something that he'd ever had a lot of practice with in his life before Adam.

"I now pronounce you husbands!" declared Margaret triumphantly. "You guys know what to do now."

Without hesitation, the pair came together into a gentle kiss that quickly built up in passion to the catcalls and cheers of their assembled group. The heat of their previous kiss at the hotel had continued over and it appeared as if they might be about to put on more of a show than anyone had expected. Fortunately, the lads managed to regain control over their baser instincts before their ardor noticeably tented the pants of their suits for the second time that day.

Turning the face the crowd, Steve thought he might very well burst with happiness. Hand in hand, he walked with his new husband down the aisle between the seats, as the guests showered them with glitter and confetti.

I'm the luckiest man alive. I never thought that I would have this chance.

* * *

A few hours later the reception was in full swing. A large marquee had been set up a few hundred yards from where the nuptials had taken place, and there stood a dozen round tables all tastefully decorated in shades of blue and gold. The happy couple had taken a few hours off from the festivities to have their photos taken while their guests enjoyed cocktails and hors d'oeuvres. They had employed the same photographer that Adam used for all the CocKed advertising, Spencer, to capture their special day. Opportunely, he was just as adept at shooting his subjects with clothing as without.

After they'd posed for seemingly thousands of photos, ranging from serious to goofy, the pair returned to the reception. The next few hours passed in blissful blur of speeches, good food, a generous amount of alcohol and rather a lot of dancing.

To the great amazement of many present, Steve took to the dance floor with gay abandon, demonstrating a surprising flexibility that seemed inconsistent with his bulky frame. All the time Steve felt the huge grin that was plastered upon his face that seemed impossible to dislodge – not that he wanted to.

The party continued well into the early hours of the morning, although the newlyweds took their leave of their guests not long after midnight, in a flurry of kisses, well wishes and sly remarks about what the rest of the night held in store. To be fair, most of the comments were perfectly within the realm of possibility given the couple's very active sex life.

Walking the short distance to the car park, the duo jumped into the limousine waiting to whisk them back to the honeymoon suite of the Grand Babylon Hotel to spend their first night as wedded men together. Once in the backseat, they were upon one another like hormone driven teenagers. Mid-kiss Steve caught the gaze of the driver, a handsome gent in his late forties with salt and pepper hair and sharp blue eyes. On another day, Steve would probably have invited him back to join them but he was too preoccupied with his love for Adam to even contemplate giving such an offer. Instead, Steve had another question in mind.

"Could you please put up the privacy screen, driver?"

"Of course, Sir," said the driver, an amused grin upon his lips.

Once the screen was up, they wasted no time, both men unable to wait until the hotel room to celebrate their union. Their wandering hands freed both their erections and were working each other up into an imminent release. Their pants were soon around their ankles and shirts were wide-open, ties askew.

As they drove onwards, the interior of the car became heated with their manly toil. Already slightly sweaty from dancing, their intermingled strong masculine scent flooded into Steve's nostrils and caused him to growl like the animal in heat he was.

Steve had a strong urge to fellate Adam but before he even lowered his head, Adam's grunted and his body stiffened as his cock erupted in Steve's thick hand. The sight of it triggered Steve's own ejaculation.

"Sorry, I came so quick," apologized Adam sheepishly. "Too worked up I guess."

"Well I did too. Besides, there's plenty of time for that later."

After cleaning up with napkins and rearranging their clothes, the pair settled into the backseat, arms around each other in a loving embrace. Adam nuzzled his head into Steve's neck.

"I can't wait to spend the rest of my life with you, Grizzly," murmured Adam.

"Right back at you, Red."

A FAMILY AFFAIR

Luke Waters steadied his hand, focused his aim and then fired off a round of shots in rapid succession. Smiling, he lowered his camera and continued to watch contentedly as his mother glided across the brightly-colored dance floor with her new husband to the strains of the bridal waltz.

She looks so beautiful and happy.

For an amateur, Luke had managed to develop reasonable photographic skills, often capturing quite striking images. This was undoubtedly due in no small part to his thriving social media addiction and the accompanying need to post an inordinate number of eye-catching photos. His dependence was such that these days his phone was practically glued to his hand; it was a wonder he managed to shower without it. That being said, a few tantalizingly wet shower selfies had made an appearance on his various profiles.

Gotta give my fans what they want!

Taking advantage of his photographic eye, Luke's mother, Holly, had appointed him unofficial photographer for the evening. He didn't mind in the slightest and had been happily snapping away since the nuptials a few hours beforehand. The ceremony itself had been sweet and informal, with the two exchanging heartfelt vows that they'd written individually, although Luke knew his mother had had quite a big input in her soon-to-be-husband's writing. After several years on her own, following the death of Luke's father, Holly was somewhat used to getting things done the way she wanted them and thankfully her new husband, Glen, had been more than happy to oblige. Indeed, he'd even lost about fifteen pounds before the wedding due to her dietary influence. Her insistence on healthier eating was understandable given that her first husband had died from a massive coronary – mostly brought about by his excess weight and sedentary lifestyle.

Momentarily looking away from the couple, Luke's eyes scanned the backyard, taking in all the cheerful faces of the crowd as they watched the freshly minted Mr. and Mrs. Taylor spin about the dance floor. It warmed Luke's heart to see his mother looking so radiant and he had to admit that they made quite the handsome couple. Mr. Taylor looked pretty dapper in his charcoal-gray suit and the brand-new Mrs. Taylor was picture perfect in a tailored royal-blue dress that complimented her buxom figure and lighter coloring. Her normally wild brunette curls had been tamed into a flattering updo style and her hazel eyes sparkled with joy as she twirled about the dance floor.

Placing them together, one wouldn't think Luke and his mother were related, as both Luke and his older brother, Todd, very much resembled their father. The brothers were almost carbon copies of one another with their strongly Nordic features – crystal-blue eyes, tall and lean builds, and mops of shaggy blond hair…although Todd's was prematurely tinged with gray.

For their second time around, neither of the newlyweds had wanted a grand wedding – as they'd both had previously – much preferring to keep it low-key. And so it had remained, a somewhat simple affair, with the marriage and reception both hosted in the back garden of the Waters' family home, attended by an intimate crowd of family and close friends. The yard was fairly spacious, like most in this particular spot of the suburbs, and fairy lights had been strung all throughout the shrubbery giving the area an almost-enchanted glow. A pleasant, late summer evening breeze carried the fragrant, intermingled bouquet of jasmine and lavender around the assembled guests.

The food was a joint effort, with members of the two families pitching in to help make the day special. Fortunately, there'd been a great deal of consultation as to the menu, so they ended up with a varied and deliciously well-matched meal, rather than the usual ten potato salads and a lone suspicious-looking tuna casserole. Luke's contribution had been the wedding cake, which admittedly had been bought from a patisserie in the city, but his lack of culinary prowess made it the more preferable option by far. The patisserie in question – Dom's Delights – was right next door to Luke's gym and he'd often sampled their heavenly pastries after a strenuous workout. Even though they didn't usually do such orders, Luke was on friendly terms with the strapping Greek-god-like owner and had convinced him to turn his talents to the much larger project. The result had been a mouth-watering, three-tier, chocolate work of art that many of the guests had marveled at on their way past the dessert table.

"Drink?" offered Luke's boyfriend, Damien, from the seat next to his.

"You know me so well."

"Back in a sec, beautiful."

Watching him walk away to the small bar that had been set up on the patio at the back of the house, Luke couldn't but help but admire the view. Damien looked resplendent in his navy-blue suit, especially the way his snug pants cradled his derriere.

Damn, that ass!

His boyfriend was of a similar muscular build to Luke but his eyes were a much darker shade of blue and his ruffled jet-black hair and darker coloring proclaimed the Persian heritage of his mother. Together, they made an arresting pair.

I'm so lucky to have him.

* * *

As Luke waited for his boyfriend to return, his thoughts turned back to their initial meeting barely a year ago, on a similarly pleasant summery evening. Their paths had first crossed at Sanctuary – a popular gay club located in a deconsecrated cathedral in the heart of Port Davinica and where Luke happened to work as the bar manager.

The work was quite different from his former profession as a financial analyst but while the pay had been good, after five years in the field, the long hours and often ruthless manner of it all had lost its appeal. Realizing that his passion laid elsewhere, Luke had reinvented himself as a simple barman. One of his former fuck-buddies, Joseph – an ebony beauty with a bodybuilder physique, striking good looks and a creatively nasty streak when it came to fucking – was the club manager and had gotten him the job. Luke was quite grateful as the position was highly sought after. The access to hot men and money to be gained in tips – the bartenders' gloriously skimpy outfits often encouraged generosity – made it a dream job for a good many horny, young gays.

Here, Luke discovered that he had quite the flair for cocktails and in his two years of bartending he'd become the proud creator of the bar's most popular drinks: Bad Influence, Mischief Makers and the Goddamn! His artistic spirit and hard-working attitude had seen him swiftly rise to his current position of manager. While Luke enjoyed his work, it had awakened a new ambition and he now dreamed of owning his own bar – hopefully with as many gorgeous men as his current employ.

At the time, Luke had enjoyed a rather sybaritic lifestyle, bedding any number of willing men, although none had progressed further than the status of recurring playmate – strictly without any emotional entanglement. When he'd first locked eyes with Damien, however, the connection had been immediate. There was something about the man's swarthy good looks that caught Luke's eye and the buff body highlighted by his tight blue t-shirt and fitted jeans certainly added to the attraction. A surge of interest flowed from his eyes and raced towards to his crotch, with a slight fluttering in his heart along the way.

Throughout the evening, Damien came back to the bar repeatedly, waiting patiently to the side if Luke wasn't available straight away. Due to the job, Luke was no stranger to good-looking men flirting with him, whether for free drinks or something more carnal in nature. Mostly, he was happy to oblige, as more often than not he was repaid for his trouble with interest. It was after Damien's third visit to the bar, and Luke had handed him yet another Mischief Maker, that the pair finally began to speak.

"Thanks, beautiful. I'm Damien by the way." His voice practically purred with interest. "What time do you get off?"

Damien's pleasing baritone gave Luke a tingling sensation that hurtled downwards and caused a stirring in his underwear.

"Luke…and whenever you give me a helping hand." Luke replied cheekily.

"I'll be back a little later then."

And with that, Damien sauntered off towards the dance floor, throwing one last sultry look over his shoulder just before he disappeared into the crowd, leaving Luke to get back to work. Between serving customers, Luke chatted with his best friend, and his assistant bar manager, Thomas, a classically-handsome man with shoulder-length brunette hair, sharp hazel eyes and a tall, well-built frame.

"Looks like you've got an admirer."

"And you have several," countered Luke, gesturing to the gaggle of twinks by the far end of the bar who couldn't have been more obvious in their interest if they'd stripped naked and prostrated themselves on top of the bar.

"Much prefer to play with yours."

"Maybe you can have him when I'm done then."

"Wouldn't be the first time I've had your cast-offs but if you were any kind of friend you'd just offer to let me tag team him with you."

Thomas gave a good-natured laugh and gave Luke's buttocks a firm squeeze before moving off to serve a heavy-set drag queen, who was impatiently signaling for attention with her blood-red talons.

Around an hour later, it was time for Luke to finish up. He was pleased to see Damien waiting off to the side, his gaze very much fixed upon the bar. So, logging out of the register,

Luke happily handed control of the bar over to Thomas, whose fan club of twinks had been replaced with a muscle bear who looked like he could have eaten them all.

"Alright, trouble, I'm off. You right?"

"Yeah, I'm sure we handle anything they need." Damien arched his left eyebrow in most wicked manner. "Have fun with that tall, dark gent of yours."

"Oh, I intend to, my friend."

"Good, good. And I expect it to hear all about it tomorrow, you filthy cockgoblin."

Luke adored their Sunday evening catch-ups where they compared notes on their respective sexploits over Indian takeout and red wine.

"Don't worry, you know I'll describe every last pump. You gotta get your thrills somehow."

The friends shared a comfortable hug goodbye and amicably parted ways. After throwing one last glance at his reflection in the mirror above the register, to check that his hair was still perfectly tousled, Luke came out from behind the bar. He walked straight over to where Damien was standing and planted a heavy kiss upon his plump lips that lasted a good minute or so. Breaking apart, Luke grasped Damien by the hand and led him along the side of the main dance floor that was heaving with merry revelers. They continued on to the far left corner where a staircase led down to the former crypt, which now housed a thriving backroom with many gentlemen in various states of undress doing all sorts of wonderfully unspeakable things to one another.

Upon entering the crypt, the amorous pair was enveloped by the heat generated by all those men at play and the unmistakable heady scent of masculine exertion. Still taking the lead, Luke pulled Damien towards an alcove at the side and the lads were soon locked in another passionate embrace. The kissing was accompanied by their roving hands, which grasped and clutched at one another, rendering their clothing askew, as their excitement grew more evident. Fingers unbuttoned jeans, explored underwear and fondled solid erections, all the while their tongues dueled between their mouths in an eager battle for supremacy. Even with the strong odor of sex around them, Luke could still smell the intoxicating musk of Damien's cologne – an interesting mixture of oak and burnt vanilla – as they kissed.

Due to the cramped conditions, the occasional strange hand wandered over their bodies, as they writhed against one another. After a while, Luke decided he'd rather not share his conquest and determined a chance of venue was in order.

"I know somewhere a bit more private," he whispered into Damien's ear.

"Sounds good to me."

They both quickly tucked themselves back into their jeans and taking his hand again, Luke directed Damien back upstairs to the main floor, grabbing a handful of condoms and lube sachets from one of the dispensers on the way. Once upstairs, they passed through a dark metal door marked STAFF ONLY directly behind the DJ podium. This opened into the stairwell for a spiral stone staircase, which in turn led up to the roof of the cathedral. After a few minutes of steady climbing, the duo arrived, breathing heavily, at the small terrace that had been set up for the staff to relax between shifts and sun-baking during the warmer months. Indeed, Luke and Thomas had spent many an afternoon working on their all-over tans, although his best friend always went much browner than Luke due to his Spanish roots.

Amongst the turrets there were several planter boxes with a variety of flowers that gave the rooftop a colorful aspect as well as an agreeable, flower-scented ambiance. The heat of the night was tempered by a light breeze that also cooled the sweat on their skin from their ascent to the roof.

"The view is incredible," remarked Damien, as he took in the twinkling lights of the city around them.

"Yeah, it is," agreed Luke, although his eyes were firmly fixed on Damien.

While it was hardly the first time that Luke had had sex on the terrace – there had been several *team-bonding* sessions with Thomas and the other barmen – he'd never before brought a stranger up there. There was just something about Damien that felt different, although Luke was unable to put his finger on it. Luckily, he had plans for his fingers in the meantime.

Coming together again, their kissing resumed with an animal-like ferocity. Frantic hands soon succeeding in stripping each other down, so that the pair were standing bare-ass naked on top of the cathedral, their clothes scattered haphazardly around them. Dropping to his knees, Luke couldn't contain his hunger any longer and eagerly devoured Damien's thick, seven inches, burying his face in the lightly-clipped bush of dark hair at the base. His right hand reached up and took a hold of the dangling ball sack, gently tugging on it as he capably worked the shaft with his mouth and throat. With his other hand, Luke gripped Damien's right hip and pulled him closer, encouraging his playmate to pound his face.

Taking the hint, Damien clutched onto Luke's head, holding it in place as he repeatedly thrust himself forward, battering into the wonderfully warm mouth before him. Beads of sweat formed on his brow and the perspiration began to run down his face and drip onto his chest, trickling its way down to where Luke was busily working away.

After a few minutes of feasting, Luke broke away from his delicious treat and led Damien over to one of the flat, wide, wooden benches at the side of the terrace. Luke knew from previous experience that they were rather practical for the activities he had in mind. Guiding Damien onto his back, Luke then climbed on top of him, maneuvering himself into a sixty-nine position, not that Damien appeared to object. If anything, the grin upon his face showed just how much he approved of the plan, as did the way he enthusiastically took Luke's cock down his throat as soon as he was in position, although he did pause to nibble on Luke's generous foreskin first.

As he sucked, Luke moved his fingers down towards Damien's tight hairy hole. He pushed and prodded at the rosebud before slowly working just the tips of his digits inside, using the sweat that had built up between the cheeks for lubrication. Luke appreciated the way Damien's hole clamped down and then released his fingers, letting them enter slightly further each time. This continued on for quite some minutes as both men continued to fellate each other to the best of their abilities and considering the practice they'd both had they were damn-near experts. Soon Luke had two fingers knuckle-deep inside his new friend, grazing back and forth over his pleasure button, causing Damien to squirm in delight as his muffled moans rang into the night.

After a few more minutes of his precise handiwork, Luke was hankering for something deeper. Breaking away, leaving Damien on his back with his legs in the air, Luke went to his jeans and grabbed the necessary supplies to suit up and slide in. He walked back over to the waiting Damien and stood right between the raised muscular legs, he let the ankles rest upon his broad shoulders before he placed his sheathed cockhead at the moist entrance. Registering the unmistakable look of need in Damien's eyes, Luke began to push, enjoying the sensation of the dark, puckered entrance opening up to let him inside. He kept sliding his member slowly forward; moving it in circular motions as it gradually filled the velvety passage, inch-by-inch, edging ever closer to the base. Reaching forward, Luke's fingers latched onto Damien's erect chocolate-brown nipples, lightly tweaking them as his cock continued to load into the silky tunnel.

Damien gasped as Luke finally slid into the hilt, reaching up to pull his playmate down into a long languid kiss as he ground his hips into him. His hands reached up and raked down Luke's back until they reached the round globes of his ass, pulling him in closer, in an apparent effort to get him even further inside.

Ever the obliging lad; Luke started to pump, taking long strokes to fully impale his companion deeper with every plunge. Luke pounded away, turned on by the way Damien lifted his hips to meet each thrust. The chemistry between the pair sizzled, their bodies working together as one, towards the goal of mutual satisfaction.

After a while, Luke changed positions, roughly flipping Damien onto his stomach before plowing him in earnest once more. He slapped the sides of Damien's firm, round buttocks, as he hammered into them, his member jabbing and exploring deep. Growls and grunts of enjoyment issued forth from both the lads, as their straining bodies glistened with the effort of their play.

From here, the action moved from the bench to up against the left turret, to the ground and back again. The twosome took turns to be cocked, Luke taking full advantage of the fact that Damien was as versatile as he.

Eventually, their adventure came to an end. Dawn was beginning to break, bathing the city in a pleasant pink glow but it also meant that Luke's coworkers would start drifting up after their shifts finished, and again Luke didn't particularly feel like sharing Damien…for the moment, at any rate.

Neither of the lads had yet blown, even though they had been close on a few occasions. Luke wanted to last as long as possible and it appeared that Damien was of a like mind. Returning to their starting point on the bench, Damien was once more on his back wanking furiously as Luke battered into his ass. Luke could see by the way Damien's body had tensed up and his near constant moaning that he was close. Kicking into an even higher gear, Luke was determined to fuck the load right out of Damien. Moments later, his efforts were rewarded as Damien shuddered and then erupted; spraying his thick, white seed upwards onto his heaving chest, a few drops even landing on his stubbled chin.

Once Damien had finished spurting, Luke pulled out and jacked himself. Only a handful of strokes were needed before he too exploded, his cream splattering onto Damien's muscular chest and mixing with the other load. Exhausted, Luke bent forward and ran his tongue along Damien's chin to lick up the spots of seed. Normally, Luke liked – not loved – the taste of cum, but that was something in the tangy flavor of Damien's that had him clamoring for more. Leaning down, Luke took Damien's sticky, cockhead into his mouth and sucked the remnants right out of the tip. Understandably, Damien gasped and grabbed tightly onto the back of Luke's head and shoulders, holding him in close.

Satisfied that he'd drained Damien dry, Luke then moved onto the bench beside him. Turning to face him, Luke tenderly stroked Damien's face and gave him a gentle peck on the lips.

"That was awesome, thanks."

"My pleasure, kind Sir."

They lay there just holding each other in a naked embrace, neither seeming in a rush to let go. The first rays of sunlight began to strike the spire of the cathedral, lighting the charcoal-gray stone.

"We should probably get dressed before anyone else comes up here." There was a slight apprehension to Luke's tone that was slightly at odds with his usual cocky persona. "Don't suppose you want to come back to mine?"

I really hope he says yes. Why am I so nervous?

In response, Damien gazed at Luke with a puckish glint in his deep, blue eyes.

"Thought you'd never ask."

A sense of relief flooded through his body and Luke couldn't help but to smile widely. Retrieving their clothes from where they had fallen, the pair hurriedly dressed themselves before making their way back downstairs, out of the club and straight into a waiting cab.

Fifteen minutes later, they were safely inside Luke's apartment; their clothes happily discarded again. The nakedness persisted for the rest of that day, as the lads continued to commit all manner of delightfully wanton acts in their ardent desire to please one another.

* * *

"Earth to Luke, you receiving me?"

Luke's attention was brought back from his happy reminiscing about Damien, by the sound of his cousin Timothy's voice.

"Yeah, sorry, I was just thinking…pleasant thoughts," he replied, still smiling at the remembrance.

"I bet you were, you dirty little boy," teased Timothy.

"Who you calling little?" Luke winked suggestively. "Besides, it's not like you're any better."

The cousins smiled knowingly at one another and a silent truce appeared to have been called. The pair had always gotten along rather well, which was unsurprising given they were the same age and shared similar interests; in particular, a love of handsome men. Indeed, they were more like brothers than cousins and at times Luke felt far closer to Timothy than his actual brother. Over the years, they had helped each other navigate the tricky process of accepting their sexuality, revealing their hidden preferences to each other long before they'd been brave enough to tell their family. Sitting beside Timothy was his husband, Miles, a strapping specimen of manhood with a powerful build and dark beguiling features. Admittedly,

Luke had been a tad envious of his cousin when he'd first met Miles.

Grrr…so my type.

Seated opposite Luke was his paternal grandmother, Dr. Evelyn Waters, her intelligent blue eyes taking in the scene and a friendly grin upon her lips. Luke adored her wholeheartedly and she had been a godsend for both Luke and Timothy helping them both through the process of coming out. Their grandmother had always been a beacon of open-mindedness.

Curiously, there were quite a few members of Luke's father's family in attendance, as his mother had remained close to her former in-laws. If truth be told, she regarded them as her family still. To be fair, it wasn't all that astounding, as Holly had no biological family apart from her children. She had been an only child and her parents had been killed in a terrible car wreck when Holly had been at college, so she'd been ever so happy to marry into a comfortingly large family of brothers, sisters and cousins. Even though they all undoubtedly continued to miss Luke's father, Charles, everyone appeared quite willing to welcome Glen into the fold.

"Here you go, Mister." Damien handed Luke a glass of champagne as he sat back down at the table. "What did I miss?"

"Nothing, my dear. Thanks for the refreshment."

They clinked their glasses in the traditional celebratory fashion, eyes locked as the rims touched. Just then the Maid of

Honor, Denice, a slender woman with kind brown eyes and short, spiky, vibrant scarlet hair, paused by their table.

"Doesn't she look wonderful?" she asked, nodding towards the happy couple.

Denice had been Holly's best friend for well over thirty years and had been Maid of Honor at both her weddings. Luke had always liked her, as she had been the fun aunt growing up, spoiling both him and his brother rotten when their parents weren't looking. Luke suspected that her indulgence of them was possibly due to her being unable to have any children of her own, following a destructive bout of cancer in her youth.

"Yes, you did a fantastic job, Auntie Denice," complimented Luke.

The Maid of Honor had offered her beauty services – she was quite a skilled make-up artist and hairdresser – to the bridal party as part of her wedding gift.

"Thanks, Lukey. It's so good to see her so happy again."

"Yeah, it is."

"You boys having a good time?"

"Of course! It's been a wonderful day, everything's gone so well." Luke's sentiment was supported by Damien's bright smile.

"Well, must move on, need to keep being social and all that, but I expect a dance later young man!"

"Yes, Auntie Denice." Luke voice was warm with affection as he turned back his gaze to the newlyweds.

I'm so glad Mom found Glen. She deserves a second chance of happiness.

Their romance had been quite some years in the making. In actuality, Holly and Glen were high school sweethearts who'd parted ways because of their college choices being a country apart. The two had lost touch over the years, as is usually the case, and had only reconnected at their fortieth high school reunion. From there they had kept in regular contact and after about three months their relationship had rekindled into its former romantic state.

To be honest, it had been awkward for Luke to start with, seeing his mother with another man, as she'd not even vaguely entertained the idea of dating during the ten years since Luke's father's untimely demise. His initial reaction left Luke feeling something of a lost little boy.

He's not my Dad!

Fortunately, Luke managed to put his selfish feelings aside, after talking things over with his grandmother, who helped him to realize that his mother's happiness was ultimately more important. After all, he didn't want her to be alone forever and he'd occasionally worried about his mother in the intervening years. Despite her brave façade there was still an aura of sadness about her that never quite went away…well, not until she had started seeing Glen.

Like his mother, Luke's new stepfather had also lost his spouse. Talia, his late wife, had succumbed to bone cancer some years beforehand. So, they were both painfully aware of what it was like to unfairly lose a great love. Things had all been going so well with the lovebirds until they had become serious enough about their relationship to introduce their families to one another, where they had run into something of an unexpected problem.

* * *

Around six months beforehand, not long before Christmas, Holly and Glen had organized an afternoon tea for the two families to properly meet in a pleasant relaxed setting. What could be possibly better than bonding over scones and tea?

The chosen venue was The Gardens, a popular restaurant situated on the top floor of the Grand Babylon Hotel with unobstructed views out over the city, a reputation for mouthwatering food and impeccable service. Their afternoon tea was considered one of the best in the city – the Internet was awash with spiffing reviews – as they had a wide selection of Mariage Frères tea on offer and a decadent spread of scrumptious sweet and savory treats to accompany them.

The temperature outside had been hovering at the underside of zero all day and it would be safe to say that the diners were generally glad to be safely tucked away from the chilly December air. From inside the cozy warmth of the restaurant, the view through the large windows of the snow-dusted cityscape had an almost magical, fairytale quality to it.

Last to arrive, Luke was all in a rush and sweating in his electric-blue parka in spite of the cold. He'd finished work rather late, due to Thomas calling in sick with a nasty touch of food poisoning, and had consequently slept through his alarm. Fortunately, his apartment was within walking distance of the hotel, so Luke was able to get himself ready and to the restaurant only ten minutes after their reservation.

Everybody was already seated and waiting, so Luke quickly deposited his parka at the coat check, straightened his clothing and gave himself a once over in the large gilded mirror by the entrance. Luke was all too mindful of the chastising he'd receive from his mother if he turned up looking disheveled. He could almost hear her disproving tone.

"Appearances are important, Luke."

Satisfied that he'd pass muster, he then made his way over to their large round table right by the window. As Luke approached, he recognized his mother, grandmother, brother and future stepfather but there were also a man and a woman, both dark-haired, seated together with their backs to Luke. He figured it must be Glen's adult children, although he didn't really know anything about them, apart from the fact they were around his age and lived in Port Davinica.

A nagging feeling of unease flitted around Luke's chest and stomach as he strode towards the table but he hadn't the faintest idea why. He greeted his family with the customary kisses of affection, apologizing for his lateness as he went. It wasn't until Luke turned around to meet Glen's children, however, that he realized what his subconscious was trying to tell him.

"Luke, I'd like you to meet my kids, Amanda and…" began Glen.

"Damien?" uttered Luke in disbelief.

I've been fucking my potential stepbrother!

"Do you two know each other?" asked Holly.

"Yes…we've been…we met…" sputtered Luke.

"Oh my God! Is this the guy?" exclaimed Amanda in a high-pitched squeal to her brother. "Good job!"

"Mandy!" Damien berated his sister with a look of exasperation contorting his face.

He told his sister about me? He must really like me. Why did he have to be Glen's son? I guess that's the end of that, then.

It took a few moments for the rest of the table to catch on, causing a babble of voices to break out at once.

"Oh dear," muttered Luke's grandmother.

"What?" Amanda huffed, her hourglass figure straining against her snug, cherry-red dress. "How was I supposed to know not to say anything?"

"Luke, what does she mean? Are you and he?" questioned Luke's mother.

"Can we please talk about this later?" The begging timbre of Luke's voice was very much broadcasting his inner turmoil.

This is just a horrible, horrible dream. Any moment I'll wake up in bed with Damien and we'll laugh at the stupidity of it all. As if I could be so unlucky to be fucking my…

"Good one, bro." Todd smirked with a touch of malicious glee.

"Ah…Damien?" asked Glen.

"Not now, Dad."

Luke took the remaining empty chair on the opposite side of the table from Damien, doing his very best not to look into his lover's apologetic and pleading eyes.

"The family that plays together…" teased Amanda, in an unsuccessful attempt to lighten the mood. "What? It's kind of funny."

"Amanda!" Glen scolded his daughter and brusquely opened his menu in front of him.

"Let's order!" suggested Luke's grandmother, in a blatant attempt to change the subject.

And so everyone studiously poured over the menus, picking out their beverages with a fierce concentration that wouldn't be out of place during a grueling session of brain surgery. Understandably, the rest of afternoon tea was filled with a stilted awkwardness. The conversation had a forced gaiety about it, while everyone carefully avoided addressing the pink elephant dancing in the center of the table.

Over the course of the next hour, Luke received many pointed looks from his family members – disapproval from his mother, amusement from his brother and gentle understanding from his grandmother. It was without doubt one of the most subdued, uncomfortable meals that Luke had ever endured. Despite the discomfort, Luke couldn't help but munch heartily on the white chocolate and fruit scones – he hadn't had breakfast and they were divine.

Thankfully, Luke was eventually released from the hellish situation and he bade a quick farewell to his family and the Taylors. After he retrieved his parka, Luke was about to walk out the heavy oak doors at the entrance to the restaurant when Damien tried to pull him aside to talk.

"Luke, wait. I know this is weird but we…"

"I just can't right now," said Luke, rushing off as fast as he could without actually running, leaving a disappointed-looking Damien in his wake.

Avoiding the elevator, lest he get trapped with any of his family members, Luke took the stairs down to the lobby. A brisk walk later, Luke forcefully shut the front door of his apartment behind him, locking out the world. Luke had never been so embarrassed in his life. Even though rationally he knew that he'd done nothing wrong, he couldn't help but feel dirty and sordid…and not in a good way.

People would judge us if they knew. Well, I guess that's over and done with. Pity, I really liked him.

* * *

Later that evening, Luke was at home watching TV and finishing off a large tub of cookie dough ice cream – his comfort food of choice – when he was roused from his melancholy by a sudden knocking at the door. Getting up to investigate, Luke looked through the peephole to see Damien standing on his doorstep.

Why did he have to come over? I'm not ready to see him.

By this point, Luke had already realized that his relationship with Damien had become more serious than one of his usually casual flings. Their playtime on the roof of the cathedral had been one of the hottest encounters he'd ever had and their sex had stayed at that same stellar level ever since. It wasn't just the sex though, as Luke found he enjoyed Damien's company a great deal, even when they managed to keep their clothes on. While they hadn't officially had 'the talk', Luke had gradually stopped playing around with his other fuck-buddies – excepting for when he and Damien shared them – each of the pair enjoying a fondness for threesomes.

It was the first time in a long while that Luke had felt something for a guy other than a hardening in his nether regions, but in light of the thoroughly unexpected revelation, Luke was still overwhelmed and unsure about what to do. He hadn't even told Thomas about what had happened, as he wasn't ready for the stream of jokes his best friend would invariably subject him to before trying to help him puzzle out the situation.

Should I let him in? But I don't know what I want to do about everything. Why does it all have to be so complicated? Don't leave him standing out there! It might be better to just end it now.

Truthfully, Luke wasn't all that surprised that Damien had turned up unannounced as he'd called several times over the course of the afternoon and sent two texts – all of which

Luke had done his very best to ignore. Now it seemed as if he was about to be forced to confront the issue regardless of whether he wanted to or not. As Luke dithered by the front door, trying to decide upon the best course of action, there was another loud knock, which caused him to jump in fright.

I've turned into a scared schoolboy! I might as well hear what he has to say.

Taking a deep breath, Luke opened the door to find a very worried-looking Damien. His bright yellow overcoat was covered in a light sprinkling of snow and his cheeks and nose had been reddened by the cold.

Why does he have to be so damn cute!

"Hi," greeted Damien, his tone conveying the same concern as his face.

"Hey."

"Sorry to turn up uninvited but I really need to talk to you and you weren't responding to any of my messages. I…I was worried about you."

"I know, I know. I'm sorry. I just didn't know what to reply. And I'm sorry about earlier, I just couldn't deal with it with everyone around and looking at us." Luke explained sheepishly. "It was all a bit of a shock really."

"You're telling me! It was the last thing I expected to happen today." Damien shifted on his feet, clearly ill at ease. "How about now, can we talk about it? Or should I go?"

A bitter conflict silently raged inside Luke's brain over that very question, but the sight of Damien looking an endearing mixture of sweet and forlorn proved to be the deciding factor.

"Sure, come in."

In a few minutes, they'd settled on the over-stuffed, toffee-colored lounge with industrial-strength, Irish coffees in hand to take the edge of the cold night air…and the awkwardness of their situation. They sat in silence, quietly sipping and looking at each other uncomfortably. It was the longest they'd spent in private without ripping each other's clothes off and violating one another. It was Luke who cracked first and gave in to his need to fill the discomfiting void with words.

"This is *so* fucked!"

"You're telling me."

"If I'd had any idea I wouldn't have…"

"Yeah, me neither."

"But…we have…and now…"

The silence returned as the pair struggled to come to terms with the unexpected, and seemingly insurmountable, obstacle in the path of their burgeoning relationship.

"Do you want to stop seeing each other?" demanded Damien suddenly.

"No…I don't know…it's just so…"

"Yes. Well, I know what *I* want."

Moving forward, Damien caught Luke off-guard by taking Luke's face in his hands and kissing him gently. Their tongues slowly circled one another, playing lightly between their mouths. Despite his natural instincts beginning to assert themselves, Luke pulled away, determined to deal with the more pressing matter of their future.

"We shouldn't…not until we…"

The rest of Luke's words were lost as Damien proceeded to kiss him again with an even greater urgency. Realizing the futility of his half-hearted protests, Luke then allowed himself to succumb to the amorous advances. This predictably led to more passionate kissing and the frenzied removal of clothing, followed by an ardent coupling right on the lounge room floor. Luke's worries fell away as he lost himself in the hungry embrace of his, for want of a better word, boyfriend.

The twosome didn't discuss the matter further that evening or indeed the next morning when they were again far too busy fornicating to care about anything other than how their bodies must continue servicing one another. It was only when Damien had left later the following evening, and Luke was once more alone with his thoughts, that the unfortunate reality of his situation reasserted itself.

Can we really keep seeing each other? What will our parents think? Is it wrong?

* * *

Despite his misgivings and a small, persistent niggling sense of doubt, Luke had continued to see Damien. Neither of the pair had broached the subject of their less-than-fraternal relationship with their families, as each had a fair idea of what

the reaction would be. Both were reluctant to end things, as they were so compatible both physically and emotionally. Indeed, their sex-charged catch-ups had become increasingly intense, perhaps due in part to the somewhat forbidden nature of what they were doing.

That being said, in some ways the pair was rather different. Career-wise, for instance, their paths couldn't be more different. While Luke reveled in the heavy social aspects of his workplace, Damien had taken after his late mother and spent his days as a chemist, in the much more sedate and sterile environment of the research and development labs of Babylon Enterprises. Initially, Luke had been a tad concerned about said research, given his strong vegetarian stance, but Damien had hastened to reassure him that there was no animal testing involved at all, even giving him a late-night tour to prove his claims. True to form, this had ended up with a hurried, and extremely satisfying, round of fucking over a handy bench in one of the smaller labs, where Damien knew the security cameras were on the fritz.

Another reason that Luke had been wary of letting Damien go was the simple fact that it was the first time since his early twenties that he had let his heart open up to the possibility of love. His last serious relationship had been with a devilishly handsome gent by the name of Tony, whom Luke had loved dearly – even after his violent side had made an appearance. It had taken several instances of verbal and physical abuse before he'd found the courage to leave. His self-esteem had taken such a battering that he hadn't allowed himself to get truly close to anyone since – until Damien.

As well as keeping his family in the dark, Luke was hesitant to share the news of the relationship with friends, afraid of being judged and thought of as a pervert – well, less than normal, at any rate. Naturally, Luke confided in Thomas, with the predicted results.

"Damn, that's so hot! Now I know why you didn't want to share him, keeping it in the family and all that."

"OK, OK. Get it all out of your system so we can talk about it properly."

"You know what, I'm pretty sure I've seen a video all about it...Family Reunion 4 – Stepbrothers in Arms."

"Aha, sure you have."

In spite of his light-hearted tone, Luke's patience was already starting to wear thin and he wasn't sure how much more teasing he'd be able to endure.

"In fact, weren't you the one that sent me the link? Must be right up your alley."

"Very funny."

"With that kind of kinky family set up, you could even have your own reality show."

"That's enough!" The gruffness of his timbre was much harsher than he'd intended and Luke immediately felt chastened by the look of hurt that appeared on Thomas' face. "Look, I'm sorry. It's just been a bit difficult, hiding it from my family. I really like Damien but I just don't know what sort of future we can have if things progress with our parents."

What if they actually get married? No, I can't even think…

"Honestly, I don't see what the big deal is. You haven't done anything wrong."

"Yeah, I know it just makes things…awkward and weird."

"Seriously though, I'll be here to support you no matter what, but I'm sure if you guys are meant to be, then everything will work itself out."

Touched by Thomas' sweetness, a small smile crossed Luke's lips and made its way up to his eyes.

"When did you become such the wistful romantic?"

"I have hidden depths."

"Really? I thought your depths had been well and truly *explored* by that bodybuilder last weekend."

"Ha! He certainly tried his hardest…I'm still a little sore!"

And from here the twosome fell back into their usual pattern of happy banter, Luke's worries banished… temporarily at least.

Resigned to keep their relationship mostly to themselves, the couple had promised not to talk about it further until there was a need. Unfortunately, this came to pass about a month after the fateful afternoon tea, on a lazy Sunday morning when Luke and Damien were lying in bed together naked, their skin and the sheets still barring traces of their steamy play from the night before. Oddly enough, they received the news within a minute of each other.

Luke's phone buzzed with a message from his mother – she often messaged instead of called over the weekend due to Luke's odd hours at the club. He had successfully fobbed her off whenever she asked about Damien but he had a sudden premonition that was going to get a lot harder. Just as he was opening the text, Damien's phone burst to life with a call.

"Hey Dad…No you didn't wake me…mmmhmm …really? That's great news! Yeah, I'm happy for you…. OK, you too. See you tomorrow. Love you, bye."

Listening in intensely, Luke had a growing feeling of dread in his stomach as to what it would be about, which was confirmed when he looked back to his phone. The pair sat in silence for a good few minutes, the screen of Luke's phone declaring what he had feared since that afternoon at The Gardens.

"What are we going to do?" bemoaned Luke. "We're going to be fucking brothers!"

"Literally."

"That's not funny."

"It kinda is. Besides, it's not really like we're actually going to be brothers. Not by blood at any rate and it's not as if we grew up together and have been having some dark incestuous relationship. We were two complete strangers who met and fell in lust."

"Yeah, but people will think it's…weird or disgusting or…"

"Fuck them! Who cares what they think? You know I enjoy what we have and that I love spending time with you. Doesn't this feel right to you?"

Damien dove under the covers taking Luke's cock down in his throat in one practiced move, causing Luke to throw his head back and wrap his legs around Damien's firm body.

"Fuck! Ah, that feels good..."

Breaking his suction, Damien lifted his head up, apparently unable to resist one more taunt.

"Right, bro?"

"Stop that!" In his annoyance, Luke roughly pushed Damien off of his groin and away to the side of the bed. "This is serious. I can't believe that you're joking at a time like this. What are we going to do?"

"I have a few ideas."

Damien jumped on top of Luke pinning him to the bed, his newly arrived erection digging into Luke's defined stomach. Determined to have a conversation about their unfortunate predicament, Luke struggled to free himself from Damien's grip but his boyfriend was in a much stronger position, having braced himself against the large mahogany bed head.

Why can't he see the problem? Doesn't he care about what'll happen to us? How can he be so blasé about it all?

No matter how hard he tried to push Damien away, Luke was still firmly held in place by the muscular embrace. Normally, it was a feeling he rather enjoyed but not when he needed to deal with the potential end of their relationship.

"How can you be so turned on right now?" demanded Luke incredulously.

"Because you're fucking hot and I want you."

To prove his point, Damien moved forward and kissed Luke ferociously, the solid manhoods rubbing roughly together as their bodies pressed hard against each other. Regardless of his want to talk, Luke's other desires began to take hold, his loins practically screaming for attention – they could be ever so demanding at times.

"We shouldn't…we need to talk…this isn't…"

Luke's protests became increasingly feebler, as Damien licked and bit his way down the body beneath him. Eventually, Luke fully yielded to his natural instincts, suddenly spinning around and restraining Damien on the bed instead; attacking him back with equal vigor.

The room was soon heavy with the aromatic scent of their manly toil, as grunts and sighs echoed about them. They then spent the next hour determinedly not talking, their mouths finding far better uses than stressing about their quandary. Giving in to his yearnings, Luke enthusiastically savored every touch and thrust.

After they were done, each of the couple collapsed back onto the bed, exhausted from their sport and soon drifted back off to sleep, contentedly wrapped up together in one another's arms.

* * *

Choosing to live in a slight state of denial, Luke relished his time with Damien with only the occasional sliver of guilt – usually whenever there was something wedding-related to attend to – piercing his blissful cocoon of sex and merriment.

Unfortunately, it was only a matter of time before familial obligation threatened to derail their blossoming relationship. Things came to a head when Luke had met up with his mother to go shopping for *The Dress*. The wedding was still three months away but she wanted to have everything organized well in advance – she did so very much like to plan. She had tried on several dresses over the past few weeks and had whittled the choices down to a final three. His mother had invited Luke along to help decide, as she admired his sharp sense of style, unlike that of her other son who often looked like he'd been dressed by a colorblind clown that he'd somehow mortally offended.

Trying his best to suppress the guilt over his secret relationship, Luke found himself sitting on a comfy couch in front of the change rooms, next to his grandmother – who'd also been brought in for her stylistic input – waiting for his mother to materialize in her third possible outfit. The boutique in question was his mother's favorite – Stylish Affairs – a popular store with ladies of a certain age, located in the downtown shopping district. They carried a wide range of flattering outfits for the more mature customer, allowing them to still bask in their femininity without simply resorting to shapeless gowns with grandmotherly-floral prints. Another sign of the attentiveness to their customers was the lack of harsh fluorescent lighting anywhere in the store, coupled with the faintest soothing hint of lilac in the air. The atmosphere was one of tranquility; a safe haven in which to do one's shopping.

Happily seated, with complimentary glasses of rosé in hand – yet another reason it was Holly's favorite – they were being doted on by Roxanne, a willowy platinum blonde, with porcelain white skin and attentive eyes that were a dark, almost violet, blue.

The red curtain of the cubicle was swept aside and Holly emerged in a most becoming sparkly emerald dress, doing a girlish twirl as she approached them.

"So, what do you think? Too much?"

"I think it's wonderful," said Luke's grandmother. "Just beautiful."

"Luke? Can you stop looking at your phone, please?" Despite her smile, there was a certain tenseness to Holly's tone. "Thoughts?"

Looking up from reading a recent text, Luke couldn't keep the broad grin off of his face.

"I like it! You'll definitely be the center of attention."

"And who has got you smiling like that, my boy?" Luke's grandmother inquired, her voice humming with curiosity.

"No one." Luke hurriedly shoved his phone into his pocket. "So, which is your favorite, then?"

His unsubtle attempt to change the subject failed miserably.

"It's not like you to be so secretive."

"Ooooh, look Evelyn he's getting all shy." Holly chimed in, obviously enjoying teasing her son. "Come on just tell us who it was."

Nosiness is obviously catching.

"You guys don't have to know everything." Despite Luke's best efforts to keep things lighthearted, an annoyed edge had crept into his timbre. "Go try the blue on again, I think it's the best."

A look of confusion clouded Holly's face, but was suddenly replaced by one of understanding, followed in short order by one of annoyance.

"It's not *Damien*, is it?"

"It's not any…I don't want to talk about it, OK? You need to finish trying on the dresses so you can decide. You're the one who wanted everything sorted by today. I vote the blue one. What do you think, grandma?"

I really don't want to do this now…or ever.

His mother, however, was not so easily deterred.

"Please tell me that you're not still seeing him?"

The moral judgment sounded heavy in her tone and irked Luke to no end. He considered lying to just make the whole mess go away but was overcome with a sudden wave of resentment and decided to just admit the truth.

"Fine! Yes, I am."

"How could you? He's going to be your brother, for goodness sake!"

"No, he's not. He'd only be my stepbrother, so there's no need to go so worked up."

"It'll make the wedding uncomfortable…for everyone."
Bridezilla has appeared!

"For you maybe, but not for me and who cares what people will think. I truly want to be with him!" Luke declared defiantly. "We're not hurting anyone, so maybe you should just butt out and let me lead my life how I wish."

"Perhaps, this is a conversation best suited for a more private setting," interjected Dr. Waters, apparently conscious of the increasingly uncomfortable-looking Roxanne hovering in the background.

Ignoring the grandmotherly words of wisdom, the mother and son continued their discussion, their voices rising to match their mounting indignation.

"Are you trying to sabotage my happiness?"

"Yes, Mother. I organize my love life around what will upset you the most. Honestly, do you think I have nothing better to do with my time than date men who displease you?"

Roxanne, who had been hanging back the by the front counter had taken this time to discreetly exit out the back and do an impromptu stock take.

"Why must you have such awful taste? Just like with…"

"With *Tony*?" Luke practically spat the name out, his eyes felt like they were burning hot.

"I'm sorry, I didn't mean…"

How could she bring him up? It took me so long to get past all that. How dare she?

"Whatever. I'm going to go."

"Luke, please don't leave angry," beseeched Holly. "We need to talk about this."

"No, I just can't do this now. I can barely even look at you!"

"Please don't run off, Luke," called his grandmother as well. "I'm sure we can work this out."

Their pleas went unanswered, however, as Luke stormed out without a backward glance, furious with his mother and with himself for still being so sensitive when it came to the subject of Tony. His mother tried to call several times that afternoon, all of which he ignored. He wasn't ready to forgive her harsh words and he had a lot of thinking to do.

Is she right? What if I really am doomed when it comes to love? Why can't I just be happy?

* * *

After spending hours on the phone seeking comfort and guidance from Thomas, Luke spent a sleepless night, tossing and turning about what he was going to do. Either way it looked like he was going to end up ruining a relationship – either with his family or with Damien. It was an impossible choice but sadly he knew what was going to be the more likely outcome.

How can I lose my family?

That evening, Luke invited Damien over for a very difficult conversation. Arriving promptly at eight pm, Damien rapped upon the wooden door. Luke paused at the door, his hand on the lock and took a deep breath.

It'd be so much simpler if he was an asshole. Why does he have to be so damn perfect?

Opening the door, Luke had a feeling of dread rising in his stomach. It was all he could do to stop himself from slamming it shut again and running to his bedroom. Instead, he gave Damien a tight smile of welcome, who then leant forward to give him a kiss, causing Luke to clumsily pull away.

"Hey, what's wrong? Do I have bad breath, cause I have a mint if I need to freshen up?"

The smile on Damien's face momentarily weakened Luke's resolve, but he knew what he had to do.

The sooner I do this the better. But is it the right decision? It has to be.

"We need to talk."

"That doesn't sound good."

"There's no easy way to say this...I...I think we should break up."

Damien exhaled loudly and rolled his eyes in a clear sign of exasperation.

"Is this because of your mother?"

"Yeah, we had a huge fight." His misery was evident in his words. "How did you know?"

"Got a call from my dad."

"We were foolish to think that we could keep doing this without them finding out and I'm beginning to think they're right. People will find it weird and it makes things difficult for us. It's probably for the best."

Maybe I'm not meant to be in a relationship?

Defeated, Luke lowered his head, unable to meet Damien's eyes. He was soon shocked out of his self-pity party by a sudden change in Damien's tone.

"Screw everyone else! I thought you cared about me?"

"I do, but I can't live my life in the shadows. What kind of future can we have if everyone disapproves?"

"We need to stand up to them! I've already told my dad that it's my business who I date and if he wants me in his life he has to accept it. I care about you but if you aren't willing to fight for it then I guess we're done."

"It's not that simple."

"It damn well is. Either you want to be with me or you don't." Damien's handsome features were contorted in anger. "If what we have isn't enough to overcome other people's prejudice them maybe we shouldn't be together anyway."

"Damien, I'm so sorry." Luke's voice wavered with the threat of tears.

"I should go."

I'm really going to lose him. I didn't want to hurt him. What have I done?

"Please don't go like this."

"So, what? I just hang out here platonically? I don't want to be your friend! I *want* to be with you properly. Would you honestly be content to just be friends with me?"

"No…I…I don't want you to go!" Luke pleaded desperately. "I just want…"

"What? What the hell do you want?" Damien's gruff voice was full of frustration.

"I want *you*, but…"

"Then don't break up with me!"

"It's just that it's more than what other people will think. I'm scared of losing my family over this." Tears started to stream down Luke's face. "I just…I don't know what to do."

Leaning forward, Damien brought Luke into a big, warm hug. He stroked his face gently and then gave him a soft kiss on the lips.

"It's all going to be, OK," reassured Damien. "I promise."

"But how do you…"

The rest of his sentence was lost as Damien bestowed a hungry kiss onto Luke's quivering lips. As was often the case with the pair, the kiss soon turned into an even more passionate embrace and before he knew it Luke was in bed, naked on his back, with Damien between his legs pumping away – not the worst of places to be by any stretch of the imagination.

Roughly an hour later, the twosome was lying contentedly together. Their bodies were thoroughly sweaty and sticky and tangled up in the sheets.

"Still want to break up?" inquired Damien, as he gently nuzzled into Luke's neck.

"Hell no!" Luke emphasized his point with a long, loving kiss. "But all the most awesome sex in the world can't solve our problem. What the hell am I going to do about my family?"

"They'll just have to get over it, I'm not going to give you up."

"I just wish that things weren't so complicated."

"Yeah, well they are. We just have to stand our ground." Defiance practically rang off of Damien's words. "They'll come around eventually. We aren't breaking any laws, for fuck's safe."

"I know, I know."

Leaning forward, Damien took Luke's face between his strong hands and gazed deeply into his boyfriend's eyes.

"You're going to be stuck with me for a good while yet, Mister."

And with another hungry kiss round two began in earnest.

Will we be able to make it work?

* * *

As the wedding drew near, the boys remained steadfast in their decision to stay together, in the face of much parental disapproval. On the plus side, Luke and his mother were back on speaking terms, after his grandmother had intervened and played to their shared love of family. Even though both had stalwartly refused to back down, an uneasy truce had been formed. Not to say that the topic was ever far from mind, for either of them. While Luke hadn't completely forgiven his mother for her comments, they remained civil to one another – somewhat important seeing that Luke and his brother were shortly set to walk her down the aisle.

Foolishly, Luke hoped that they might make it until the wedding day without any further unpleasantness, but it was not to be. It was at a joint family dinner a few days before the wedding, when they'd gathered to put the finishing touches to the party plans that the simmering tensions flared-up once more.

"I can't believe you'd be this petty!"

The anger in Luke's words cut brutally through the air. The vexing issue was all to do with the seating plan – Luke and Damien had been purposely sat apart. It felt like a very real slap in the face and immediately got Luke's back up.

For his part, Damien was happy to just let it go, preferring to avoid the drama. It was a trait he shared with his father, who, to be honest, didn't really mind the boys' relationship as much as Holly did, but who had wisely chosen to go along with his fiancée's wishes – as he had with most things in regard to the wedding.

"Why can't we sit together?" demanded Luke. "Everyone else is sitting with their partner."

"Luke, please, not now." There was a distinct weariness to Holly's tone.

"What? I just want to sit next to my boyfriend. I really don't think it's too much of an ask!"

"It's OK." Damien was obviously trying to calm the situation with his serene, level cadence. "I don't mind where we sit, it's just a dinner."

"Damien can swap with me," offered Todd.

"You sure?"

Taken aback, Luke was slightly suspicious of his brother's generosity. It was the kindest thing Todd had done for his brother in years; covering for Luke when he'd nearly been caught out partying all night in the city when he was still in high school had been the last memorable time. That being said, he wasn't above adding to the drama on occasion.

"Yeah, of course." Todd smirked a tad maliciously. "Brotherly love and all that."

"And that's the sort of comment I want to avoid!" exclaimed Holly, clearly mortified at the thought.

It was then that a sudden clear voice of reason entered the discussion.

"For heaven's sake, they aren't doing it to spite you," declared Dr. Waters, in her most professional timbre. "They aren't related and aren't doing anything wrong."

"Thanks, grandma."

"But Evelyn, what will others *think*?" Turning back to her son she continued on in her righteous manner. "Why do you have to be so difficult? Why can't you just keep things discreet until after the wedding?"

"Because I love him!" proclaimed Luke, shocking himself just as much as anyone.

The declaration was greeted with a grand silence in the dining room, all eyes now on Luke, including Damien who was looking at him with a stunned expression.

"You do?" asked Damien, his eyes full of curious hope.

"Damn straight I do. That's why I don't want to pretend that we aren't together. I'm sorry, Mom, but I don't want to have to hide the way I feel about him, I did enough of that as a teenager."

Moving forward, Damien took Luke's hands in his and looked him squarely in the eyes.

"I love you, too."

They embraced, the rest of the world briefly disappearing as they held each other close. The strong arms encircling him made Luke feel wonderfully safe and secure.

After a tense moment, it appeared that Holly's resistance was starting to crack. The realization that the boys were committed enough to each other, as to risk the wrath of the respective families in order to be together, seemed to have penetrated her somewhat prejudiced sense of propriety.

"Alright, you can sit together," said Holly with a resigned air. Visibly attempting to relax and soften her tone, she continued. "Why didn't you tell me it was so serious?"

"I was afraid I guess, I haven't felt this way in a long time."

"Awww, it's so beautiful," squealed Damien's sister, Amanda.

"OK, let's finish wrapping these gift bags and we can eat!" announced Holly. "What does everyone want on their pizzas?"

The tension having been reduced to a mere simmer in the background again, the group swiftly accomplished the remaining tasks before all indulging in their greasy pizza dinner. The rest of the evening passed amicably enough, with Luke and Damien exchanging many a look of shared happiness throughout the evening.

I can't believe it all worked out. Maybe it'll be our wedding we're planning next, that'll make for an interesting family tree. Need to stop getting ahead of myself…dating first then who knows.

* * *

The happy couple finished their first dance and gave a gracious bow to the crowd, who provided them with a warm round of applause.

"OK, Ladies and Gents. It's time to join the happy couple on the dance floor," announced Todd, who'd been acting as the MC for the wedding.

Looking to his left, Luke smiled at Damien, who returned the look with interest.

"Would you do me the honor of a spin about the dance floor?" asked Luke.

"How could I possibly refuse such a handsome man?"

Taking Damien by the hand, Luke led his boyfriend onto the dance floor with the other couples. They came together in a loving embrace, even if there were a few raised eyebrows from those who hadn't previously known of the pairing. The couple then proceeded to dance quite closely, in a manner that was far from brotherly, but then again so were they.

This feels so right. I can't believe I ever truly questioned it.

As Luke danced cheek to cheek with Damien, his nostrils were filled with the familiar scent of oak and burnt vanilla – his crotch expanded slightly as his thoughts drifted back to that night on top of Sanctuary.

"I'm so happy to be here with you." Luke whispered into Damien's ear.

"Me too," replied Damien, as he kissed Luke lightly on the cheek. "You know, I've always wanted a brother."

Seriously? So not funny.

Annoyed by the ill-timed joke, Luke tried to push Damien away but was held tight in place by his boyfriend's well-built arms.

"What? I meant Todd." The cheeky regard upon Damien's features betrayed his mischievous intention. "I swear."

"Sure, you did. But just as well, 'cause I've all got all manner of non-familial things planned for you later."

"Looking forward to it."

The rest of the evening passed by in a pleasant blur of speeches, cake cutting and much merriment. Luke's smile lasted well after the party and was still plastered on his face a few hours later when he and Damien were back in Luke's apartment, their bodies intertwined in a blessed state of mutual satisfaction. Lying there in the post-coital glow, Luke was considering a proposition that he'd been mulling over for the past few weeks.

What if he says 'no'? I've got to take the chance.

Turning on his side to face his boyfriend, Luke ran his fingers over Damien's lightly haired chest.

"So…I've got something I wanted to ask you?" he began tentatively.

"Yes! Yes! A thousand times yes! Of course, I'll marry you!" gushed Damien over dramatically, sitting up and pulling Luke into a firm hug.

"You're *so* funny."

Good thing that's not what I was going to ask.

"You mean I put out for nothing? Will no one make an honest man out of me?"

"Well, I was going to offer for us to live together in sin but if you're…"

Damien stopped his theatrics and gazed at Luke with serious intent.

"Wait! What?"

"I'm asking you to move in with me, doofus."

"Seriously?"

"Of course. I love you and want to spend as much time as I can with you. I know we haven't been together all that long but I really think we have a future and I'm ready to take the next step with you but I understand if you're not. It's just…"

Fortunately, Luke was cut off mid-ramble by a hungry kiss.

"Yes!" answered Damien when the pair broke for air a few minutes later.

"You're sure?"

"Don't make me change my mind."

"OK, OK."

And with that they fell back on the bed and proceeded to consummate their newfound level of commitment with great gusto. Their lovemaking continued on for quite some time and just before Luke drifted off to sleep, one last thought stole through his drowsy mind.

I never thought I'd be so happy.

TILL DEATH DO US

Oscar Nightingale took the white cotton, monogrammed handkerchief from his jacket pocket and began to dab at the fresh tears pricking the corners of his eyes.

I'm such a sap. Why must I always cry at weddings?

In his defense, the outdoor ceremony was rather moving and it was his youngest granddaughter, Mackenzie, getting married, after all. Over the years, Oscar had attended countless weddings but the ones for his offspring were always the most sentimental. Beside him sat his husband, Liam, who looked resplendent in a charcoal-gray suit, paired with a cobalt-blue shirt and black tie. His black patent leather shoes were buffed to perfection – so shiny one could almost see one's reflection.

I'm glad he still takes so much pride in his appearance.

Granted, Liam wasn't as sprightly as he'd been when the pair first met, as he now needed a cane to walk due to a fall a few months prior but, nevertheless, he cut a dashing figure for a nearly ninety-year-old man. Oscar placed his hand on top of Liam's but his husband didn't appear to notice, apparently too enthralled by the proceedings.

Dressed in a beautifully tailored, A-line, white dress, which showed off her nymph-like figure, and holding a small bouquet of lilacs, Mackenzie looked absolutely radiant…and Oscar couldn't have been prouder. Her brunette locks cascaded down her back and her inquisitive green eyes – inherited from her father and grandfather – twinkled with happiness.

As Mackenzie turned towards her almost-husband, Lachlan Spooner, the sunlight caught on her silver necklace. It was her 'something old' and had been given to her by Liam that very morning. It brought back many happy memories for Oscar, as he'd originally given the necklace to Liam on a trip to Paris in honor of their tenth anniversary.

The groom also looked picture perfect in a well-cut navy blue suit, a crisp white shirt and a purple bow tie – the latter chosen because of his similarly colored glasses and Mackenzie's bouquet. He was a handsome man, if somewhat bookish, with cropped raven hair and liquid brown eyes. Originally from Canada, he'd met Mackenzie barely a year and a half ago, on a skiing holiday with mutual friends in the Italian Alps. Admittedly, it was quick but Oscar was in no position to judge, having married Liam after an equally brief period of courtship.

When you know, you know.

The setting for the ceremony was right in the center of the picturesque gardens of Babylon Sunrise; a resort located a few hours outside of Port Davinica, in the heart of Christie National Park. The park itself was something of a special spot for the family, as it had been the location of a good many camping trips, hikes and picnics over the years. The fact that it wasn't overdeveloped only served to add to the beauty of the place.

The garden was the perfect venue for such a romantic event, with striking views down the valley and of the surrounding mountains. Ten rows of pristine white chairs, all fitted with plump, purple cushions for the comfort of the guests, were set up facing the stunning vista. The afternoon sun was almost overly warm but the light breeze kept everyone from overheating. The leaves of the nearby trees rustled overhead and the scent of a multitude of wildflowers, mixed in with the blooms of the resort's own flowerbeds, filled the air with a most pleasant floral bouquet. Knowing well the threat of inclement weather for outdoor weddings, the happy couple had chosen to hold it in June to reduce the risk, but there was also the provision of a suitably large function room just in case.

To transport the guests in style, and save them the hassle of driving, several luxury coaches had been hired to ferry the nearly one hundred invitees up from the city. The entire resort had been reserved for the weekend, as the festivities were planned to continue from the Friday evening cocktail party right through to the Sunday brunch. Normally, Babylon Sunrise was a popular naturist retreat for those wanting to really commune with nature but it wasn't so for this weekend – they weren't *that* close a family.

Officiating the event was Tom Young. A hefty man in his sixties with a friendly countenance and a matching disposition, he was also a long-time family friend and had actually presided over several of the family weddings over the past few decades. His experience shone through and his booming voice was heard clearly throughout the garden, as he drew to the close of the proceedings.

"You may now kiss the bride," declared the celebrant.

Eager to comply, the newlyweds sealed their marriage with a relatively chaste kiss, as the assembled guests broke into applause. Oscar clapped wildly, in between wiping away even more fresh tears and looking at his husband, who appeared to be in an equal state of heightened emotion.

Ain't love grand!

* * *

Even though the proceedings themselves had gone smoothly, there had been a spot of bother just beforehand…what would a wedding be without a dash of drama? A few hours before Mackenzie was due to walk down the aisle, Kayla – Mackenzie's mother and Oscar's ex-daughter-in-law – had come knocking on their hotel room door.

"You've got to come, Mackenzie is in a right state and only wants to talk to her Poppy Liam."

While Oscar loved her dearly, Mackenzie had always shown more of a preference for Liam – the reverse was also true…not that grandparents are supposed to have favorites. Filled with concern, Liam went to Mackenzie's aid straight away. Naturally, being equally fretful for his beloved granddaughter, Oscar tagged along. Once they reached the hallway, their ears were assaulted by the increasingly shrill voice coming from Mackenzie's room.

"I can't do it! Call everything off. It's not going to happen. This is the worst day ever. I can't believe I let everything get so far. Tell everyone to go home!"

At that moment a very worried looking maid-of-honor, Jessica, exited the room in a surprisingly becoming, Egyptian-blue, column dress. Clearly, Mackenzie hadn't subscribed to the age-old practice of putting the bridesmaids into the most unflattering outfits possible in order to guarantee her the unquestioned spotlight.

"Please talk some sense into her," begged the shapely redhead. "I'm going to get some Valium from my room just in case."

Turning on her heel, she sashayed off to the second door down on the left.

"Maybe, I'd better go in alone," offered Liam.

"I think that's best," agreed Kayla. "I need to finish getting ready myself."

Hesitant to face his slightly unhinged-seeming granddaughter, Oscar didn't object and stayed at the doorway listening in, as Liam entered the Honeymoon Suite and Kayla went off to her room at the end of the corridor. He wanted to give them a modicum of privacy.

Liam is much better at calming others down than me. I don't understand why she's acting like a spoiled brat, it's very unlike her and at twenty-six she's hardly a child anymore.

"Now, my little Seamonkey," inquired Liam, gently taking Mackenzie's hand. "Whatever is the matter?"

"I can't do it Poppy! I'm not sure I'm not doing the right thing. It's all happened so fast. What if I've made a terrible mistake? What if it all falls apart like mom and dad!"

And what a calamity that was.

Their son, Anthony, and Mackenzie's mother, had had a particularly bitter divorce and were only just back on civil terms five years afterwards.

"Well no one knows the future, Dearheart," counseled Liam, his words projecting a grandfatherly wisdom. "You may stay together forever or break up next week."

"That's not reassuring at all!" Her voice held a wavering quality that heralded the start of tears. "What am I going to do?"

"Now, now. It's not all lost. Lots of people have second thoughts before a wedding. In fact, I had cold feet before I married Pop."

"You did?"

Oscar stiffened in the doorway. The admission came as of much a surprise to him as to Mackenzie.

He what? Why didn't he tell me? I would've understood. Probably.

"Yes, I was worried that it might not work out. I mean we were crazy in love but my parents had divorced too. In the end, I decided that I just needed to have faith in the love we had together and, honestly, it was the best decision of my life. Things won't always go smoothly but the most important thing is to remember to always follow your heart."

"Your relationship is one I've always admired," admitted Mackenzie, her tone calmer than before.

"You know Pop and I had our problems too but we made it work. You never know what life will throw at you but you have the support of family and friends. Besides if Lachlan steps out of line your Aunty Susan will just have him renditioned somewhere."

Their eldest daughter, Susan, a sturdy, no-nonsense woman with piercing blue eyes and severe silver hair, was ranked quite highly in the military. Even though they joked about it, she had an aura of power about her that bordered on alarming. The pair laughed companionably together.

"Thanks, Poppy. You always know how to cheer me up."

"My pleasure, Seamonkey. Now, time to wipe away those tears and get you ready. Should I go fetch Jessica to help?"

"Yes, please, Poppy, I'm a mess!" exclaimed the bride-to-be, a tad melodramatically.

"Nonsense, you're the most beautiful girl in the world."

This brought a wide grin to Mackenzie's previously anguished countenance.

"You're biased."

"Maybe but it doesn't make it any less true. I'll be back in a jiffy!"

The exchange filled Oscar's heart with joy. As his husband passed through the doorway on his mission to retrieve the maid-of-honor, Oscar breathed in Liam's familiar woody scent – a pleasing combination of old books and his habitual aftershave.

Looking back into the room, Oscar saw Mackenzie sit down in front of the vanity and touch up her makeup, not that there was much damage to repair – thank goodness for waterproof mascara!

Leaving his granddaughter in peace, Oscar moved from the door and drifted back to his hotel room, intending on catching up with Liam before going to take their spots in the front row for the ceremony.

Even after sixty years he still surprises me.

* * *

Shortly after the ceremony, the guests were free to retire to the nearby reception area; the obligatory group photos with everyone smiling widely for the photographer had already been dispensed with. The happy couple, however, was sequestered away to pose for a series of more intimate photos.

The reception room was aptly named, Cirlesque, in that it did indeed resemble a cross between a circus and a burlesque club. The pointed circular roof was strongly reminiscent of a big top tent, while the stained-glass windows, plush velvet booths and Art Deco mirrored wooden paneling on the columns gave it a much more elegant flair.

No expense had been spared for the reception – Lachlan worked in finance and appeared intent on making the weekend fit for a princess and her subjects. The service was impeccable and friendly, and the food was scrumptious and seemingly never-ending. Before the dinner, the invitees enjoyed canapés and cocktails on the terrace, which offered a similarly spectacular view as the gardens but faced in the opposite direction towards the coast.

To the right side of the room, opposite the DJ, an open bar was in place and Oscar was pleased to note that everyone seemed to be behaving themselves – for the moment, at any rate. It helped that one or two of the more responsible guests had been charged with keeping the alcohol-fond family members in check and from causing a scene, as had been the case at one of their other granddaughter's wedding a few years ago.

Poor Daphne.

The bride had ended up in a flood of tears after a drunken, and thoroughly embittered, Cousin Frederic had launched into an unfortunate tirade during the best man's speech about how Australian immigrants were stealing jobs. Granted, his company had been bought by an Australian corporation in a hostile takeover and he'd struggled to find a job ever since. The fact that he was in his mid-fifties, and the drinking he'd taken to after losing his job, hadn't exactly enhanced his prospects. Thankfully, he appeared to be much more together these days but there were still one or two relatives that needed to be regarded with a watchful eye. Nobody wanted to have to carry Great Aunt Mable up to her room after she'd had one too many gins again.

She never could handle her liquor, although she certainly knew how to party.

After an hour, Mackenzie and Lachlan made their grand entrance to a thunderous chorus of cheers and clapping. Once they'd taken their place at the bridal table, everyone else followed suit and took their seats in preparation for the dinner and speeches. Gazing over at his husband, Oscar felt a familiar surge of love and affection swell his heart. It never failed to place that special smile upon his face that was reserved for loving thoughts of his husband. While the years had turned their hair white and wrinkled their skin, their love for one another hadn't been diminished by the onward march of time. If anything, the devotion he felt for Liam had only continued to grow and deepen since their wedding day.

Admittedly, the pair was an awfully good fit for one another, and not just in the physical sense, where they did indeed excel. The twosome truly enjoyed the other's company, whether they were happy sitting side-by-side reading in their cozy library in the depths of winter, baking their bodies together at a sandy beach on a lovely summer's day or dancing topless on a podium in a packed nightclub – although there had been far less of the latter these past few decades.

Both also shared a love of the arts, Liam preferring to visit galleries and museums while Oscar favored the opera. Port Davinica had quite the thriving theatre scene and they had both belonged to the same theatre troupe – the Halcyon Players – for many years. It was a small but dedicated company that put on several productions per year, usually to favorable reviews, whose loyal bunch of patrons kept the theatre afloat. Occasionally, they put on musicals, which was where Liam excelled. He had a wonderful voice, which Oscar loved to listen to even if he was a tad jealous of the soulful baritone, as opposed to his own caterwauling. They had been in many productions together over the years and had kept in up well into their seventies. The past few years they had been more content to sit and watch the youngsters have their turn but they remained faithful patrons of the arts.

Thinking back to their first meeting, Oscar had no idea that the bookish man with the disarming smile would change his life in such a grand way. As one would expect, Oscar was wont to reflect upon the moment he'd initially set eyes on Liam all those years ago.

He's still just as handsome. How did I ever get so damn lucky?

* * *

It was nigh on sixty years ago, on a fine spring afternoon, when Liam walked into the beginner's tap class that Oscar happened to be teaching. The classes were held on the stage of the Victoria James Theatre, a small building that dated back over a hundred years and was nestled in the heart of Port Davinica in the shadow of an old, gothic-inspired Cathedral. Solomon James, a strapping man of European descent, whose family had been one of the original settlers of the city some few hundred years before, owned the theatre and happened to be the founder of the Halcyon Players.

At the time, teaching was a relatively new vocation for Oscar, as in his late teens and twenties he'd been a successful professional dancer working with different touring companies around the States, Europe and Asia. Sadly, the wear and tear of his chosen career had taken its toll on his body so he'd cut back on his freelance gigs and began teaching – tap being one of his favorite styles – to make up the shortfall in revenue.

Tying up the laces of his tap shoes, Oscar prepared to start the class when he noticed a newcomer appear in the aisle of the theatre. He was an attractive man with a lean build, wavy blond hair, warm brown eyes and tanned olive skin.

He's a bit of alright. Down boy.

"Hi there," called Oscar. "You're here for the tap class?"

The man nodded and slowly advanced further down the aisle.

"Then welcome! Come up and find a place for yourself. We're all friendly enough here…mostly." This elicited a titter of laughter from the other participants, who were all regulars. "I'm Oscar."

"Liam," replied the newcomer shyly.

"Glad to have you here. OK, let's begin!"

Throughout the class, Oscar found his attention being repeatedly drawn back to Liam, even though there were fifteen others in the class, and not just because of his lackluster dancing – Liam appeared to have three left feet and none of them managed to be in time.

His clumsiness is rather endearing.

At the end of the class, Liam waited until everyone else had left before timidly approaching Oscar.

"Thanks so much for that," said Liam, only just meeting Oscar's eyes. "I really enjoyed it."

"I'm glad to hear it. Liam, isn't it?"

Oscar couldn't fail to notice the way Liam's eyes lit up at the fact that he'd remembered his name.

"Yes, it is. Thanks, again. I gotta go."

"See you next time."

Liam scuttled off quickly but had returned faithfully for every Wednesday afternoon class over the next month. After each class Liam began to chat with Oscar for increasingly longer periods. The conversations quickly came to feel more flirtatious in nature – to Oscar at least – but he was reluctant to cross any boundaries by proclaiming his attraction first.

He's so damn cute. Yeah, but I'm his teacher. Maybe he can teach me a thing or two. Stop it!

At the end of the month, Liam came to Oscar with an inviting proposition.

"I'm really enjoying the classes, even if my feet don't seem to agree," lamented Liam. "Honestly, sometimes it feels like they belong to someone else."

"You aren't *that* bad," comforted Oscar, although the same thought had crossed his mind. "Everyone learns at their own pace."

"I know…but I…I was wondering if you give private lessons?"

I'd love to do all sorts of things with you privately.

"Sure, of course."

"That'd be awesome," exclaimed Liam with a wide grin. "I'm sure I can get there with your help."

"I'll do my best."

From here they practiced twice a week and slowly but surely Liam started to improve. All the while, Oscar did his very best to ignore the sexual tension between them – not that he had much success.

I've had all sorts of hot guys in my classes before why can't I stop thinking about him? I can't afford to get that kind of reputation. It might be worth it though.

Several weeks passed and as much as he enjoyed Liam's friendly company and passion for learning, Oscar found himself plagued by more and more sexual thoughts of his student. At times, he found it hard to concentrate on Liam's feet, when his eyes wanted to wander all over his body, particularly his alluring midsection.

In spite of his promise of self-control, Oscar's desires finally got the best of him in the middle of a private lesson. Liam had just successfully mastered a simple routine and was practically bouncing around the stage with happiness.

"Great work!" praised Oscar. "You're really getting the hang of it."

"It's all thanks to you," gushed Liam excitedly, as he moved forward and gave Oscar a very friendly hug that lingered slightly longer than necessary. "You're a very patient teacher."

The raw odor of Liam, his usual woody scent enhanced by his perspiration, filled Oscar's nostrils and sent his libido into overdrive. Unable to restrain himself any longer, Oscar turned his face towards Liam's and kissed him passionately. The kiss was returned with equal interest, their tongues dueled frantically, as their bodies pressed tightly together. Suddenly, Oscar recovered his senses and stepped back hastily, feeling ashamed of his lust-fueled actions.

Damn, that was stupid! But the kiss was so damn hot!

"I'm sorry that was unprofessional," apologized Oscar profusely. "Please forgive me?"

Instead of answering, Liam stepped forward and wrapped Oscar up in another hungry embrace. Their sweaty bodies pressed together as the pent-up passion longed for its overdue release.

Breaking away briefly, Oscar tired one last time to maintain his veneer of professionalism.

"Are you sure about this?" he questioned, albeit a tad half-heartedly. "I don't want abuse my position as your teacher."

"I won't tell if you don't," replied Liam, with impish eyes.

"Good enough."

Clothing soon littered the stage around them, as they eagerly stripped one another down. During the fervent undressing, Oscar discovered that Liam's lean body was decorated with no less than three tattoos – a flaming sun atop his right arm, a Celtic symbol on his chest and a small multicolored dragon running along his left thigh. This came as a complete surprise to Oscar, as they seemed rather incongruous with his student's more sedate scholarly appearance.

I'll have to ask him about those later.

After taking a moment to fully appreciate the pleasing sight of a naked and aroused Liam, Oscar gave into his yearning. Lifting Liam's arms, Oscar moved forward and hungrily devoured the sweaty pits, relishing the taste of the salty musk. The masculine aroma caused his cock to swell to its full seven inches and precum to drip from the tip of his mushroom head. Sinking to his knees, Oscar buried his face in Liam's crotch and wasted no time ably deep-throating the sizeable the meat he found there – he'd long lost his gag reflex – savoring the sweet taste of the juice leaking from the glans. The dance practice had made Liam's crotch particularly pungent, the pure maleness of it drove Oscar wild. His hands gripped Liam's hips encouraging the lad to pump his face, with which Liam happily complied.

Soon after, the pair fell to the floor and became lost in a whirl of mutual yearning, sucking, licking and biting, attempting to consume each other from head to toe. Naturally, this progressed into a wonderfully satisfying bout of mutual fellatio. Their slurps, grunts and moans echoed in the empty auditorium bouncing off the walls, as they put on quite the display. Oscar had never been this desperate for another man and was delighted to note that Liam appeared equally as eager.

Breaking out of their hungry sixty-nine, Liam spread Oscar's lean legs wide and then used his fingers and tongue to expertly attack the exposed, puckered entrance. Groaning at Liam's rimming, Oscar gripped the back of his playmate's head to push his face in deeper, while he continued to worship the solid manhood in his own mouth. While normally preferring to top, Oscar adored his ass being played with and wasn't opposed to bottoming for the right man…and the right cock. Through the attention Liam was lavishing on the area, it was quite clear what Liam desired and Oscar was more than happy to oblige. Moving free from the embrace, Oscar turned over onto his hands and knees, and wiggled his ass suggestively.

Taking the hint, Liam was soon on his knees behind Oscar and rubbing his engorged cockhead against the inviting entrance. The hole was already slick with saliva from Liam's rimming, so he simply began to push himself inside, causing the knob to enter with a sudden pop.

Gasping at the breech of his sphincter, Oscar forced himself to relax and accept the rest of the penetrating cock. Apparently sensing Oscar's discomfort, Liam leaned forward and nibbled the back of his neck while moving his cock in and out with slow, deliberate motions, edging inside a little further each time.

Fuck! He feels even bigger than he looks.

This went on for a good few minutes as Oscar gradually loosened up and he shortly felt Liam's hips pressing into his buttocks and their balls lightly rubbing together. After a few moments, Liam began to plow him with deep, steady strokes, his bulbous arrowhead grazing the prostate and causing Oscar's own cock to form a growing pool of precum on the wooden floor below him. Liam's hands moved forward to grip either side of Oscar's crotch as he began to pound away ferociously.

This is the hottest sex I've had in…years!

Following several delightful minutes in this position, the wooden floor of the stage was beginning to become painful on both their knees and outweigh the pleasure. Liam removed himself slowly, leaving Oscar feeling empty and in desperate need of being retaken. Maneuvering around, Liam laid on his back, allowing Oscar to start enthusiastically bouncing up and down on the solid manhood. In this new arrangement, Liam penetrated even deeper inside and sending sparks of pleasure through Oscar's straining body. With all the stimulation, Oscar soon found he couldn't hold his release off any longer. A series of primal grunts issued forth from his mouth, as his body tensed up and shook, and ejaculated in huge spurts over Liam's smooth, glistening chest.

When Oscar was spent, Liam spun them around again so that his teacher was on his back with legs spread wide. Obviously close to his own release, Liam began to hammer into Oscar's sensitive passage, causing a stream of curses and grunts of appreciation to escape his lips. Barely a minute later, Liam's breathing came in short gasps as he unloaded his hot seed deep inside of the slick passage encasing his manhood. Collapsing down, the twosome lay still together in a sweaty, sticky and thoroughly contented heap. The only sound their heavy breathing, as they held each other tightly.

After a few minutes locked in this blissful tableau, Oscar broke the silence.

"So, do you want to go out some time?"

"What do you think?" answered Liam cheekily, as he dived back in for a fresh kiss.

The pair had gone another two rounds on the stage before needing to vacate, lest actors coming in for an evening rehearsal catch them. A series of daily dates followed and they'd become an official couple a mere week later and remained together ever since…mostly.

* * *

As his thoughts returned back to the reception, Oscar looked out at his children, grandchildren and great-grandchildren, his heart swelling with love and pride at his brood. It did Oscar's spirit good to see the room full of many generations coming together for a happy occasion. They were easily his greatest accomplishment and quite the tribe with three children, seven grandchildren and now ten great-grandchildren.

At times, Oscar could scarcely believe that they were a part of him and it comforted him that the family line would continue for a few generations yet. As surprising as it seemed to him now, Oscar had initially been very hesitant to have children. In fact it was a source of contention for him and Liam in the months leading up to their own wedding. So much so, that it almost put an end to their relationship completely.

About two months before their nuptials the lovebirds were lazing in bed on a rainy Sunday afternoon, having defiled each other several times since breakfast. Liam was cuddled into Oscar, his fingers tracing along his fiancé's lightly haired, muscular chest.

"Wouldn't it be nice to have the pitter patter of little feet?" inquired Liam in a soft, dreamy voice.

Not this again. Why can't he be content with what we have?

"You've got Ralph for that," joked Oscar, gesturing towards their faithful pet sleeping in his basket in the corner of the bedroom.

"Funny. A golden retriever isn't the same as a child."

"Yeah, they're less expensive and tend to be more obedient."

"I'm serious. I really want to have kids."

"Really? Can't we just enjoy the day?" Oscar's tone became edged with irritation. "I'm over this conversation."

"But you're so great with your sister's kids," insisted Liam. "You'd make a great dad."

"It's not that I don't like them, you know that. I've just never really had the great *desire* to have my own. I'm just not sure that fatherhood is for me."

"But…"

"But nothing. I don't want to go over this again. For the moment, you and Ralph are all I need."

Suddenly, Liam jumped out of the bed, his face contorted in anger.

"Well, it's not all I need. This is important to me. Why can't you see that?"

Afraid of where this was heading, Oscar resisted the urge to become defensive and tried to remain calm.

"Just come back to bed, there's no need to get so upset."

"Don't tell me what to feel. This is important! I don't think I can be with someone, who doesn't want the same things."

"What are you saying?" demanded Oscar, his urgent tone broadcasting his rising panic.

Looking away, Liam took a few moments to answer. His voice held traces of tears.

"I…I think maybe we should hold off on the wedding until we both know what we want."

Leaping from the bed, Oscar grabbed a hold of his fiancé.

"Liam, I don't want to lose you!"

"And I don't want that either but this is something that I can't back away from." Easing free of Oscar's grip, Liam started to get dressed. "I'm going to stay at my parents place for a few days. We can *both* have a think about the future."

After Liam left, Oscar retreated back to bed and stayed wrapped up in a cocoon of blankets, misery and regret. Over the next few days Oscar was a distracted mess as he replayed the issue in his mind, wrestling with the decision. He called and left messages for his fiancé but received nothing but silence in return. The worry even affected his work, with Oscar canceling his classes, much to the chagrin of his students, as he just couldn't focus on anything else.

Would being a dad be so bad? I'm not sure I'm cut out for it. But it's so important to Liam. It is such a huge commitment though…so is marriage and I'm ready for that. How can I know what's right?

By the end of the week, Oscar had come to a decision so he'd called Liam back to the apartment to talk over dinner. The conversation was somewhat stilted, as they made their way to the couch and sat down. Suddenly, with tears in his eyes, Liam dived through the awkwardness, apparently having decided the likely outcome.

"I think I know what you're going to say and I'm sorry but…"

"Liam, stop," interrupted Oscar gently. "Just listen. You're the most important thing in the world to me and if this is what you truly want, then I'm prepared to give it a go."

A look of pure joy filled Liam's handsome features.

"You're sure?"

"Yeah. I am. But I do have some conditions."

"What are they?" asked Liam, with a slight wariness.

"I'll commit to having *one* child." Seeing Liam's crestfallen expression, Oscar hastened to clarify his position. "I'm not saying that we can't have any more but I need to see how we cope…how *I* cope before agreeing to having more."

"OK, that's fair. What else?"

"I don't want to do the whole suburban, white picket fence thing, where our whole world revolves around the PTA and we get old and fat. I want to raise them in the city and not lose our old lives completely."

"I can deal with that."

"And one more thing."

"Yes?"

"We have to give them normal names without weird pretentious spelling."

A broad smile began to spread on Liam's features, obviously realizing that he'd gotten what he wanted.

"Done!" cried Liam happily. "I promise you won't regret this."

A passionate embrace soon followed and the tensions of the past week found much more pleasurable ways to work themselves out. Afterwards, as the results of their play dried slowly upon their slick skin, Oscar couldn't help but have one last lingering doubt.

I hope I'm doing the right thing.

Of course, when they'd had their daughter Susan three years later, Oscar had fallen in love from the first moment he held her in his arms. And she soon became a proper Daddy's girl. Admittedly, there were missteps along the way and many a night when Oscar though he might pull out his hair in frustration but as they welcomed two more children into their lives, Oscar never regretted changing his mind.

Best decision I ever made.

* * *

Surrounded by his family, Oscar was reminded of all the happy years they'd spent together, full of love and laughter, various pets and an altogether messy, happy life. The house had always been full of noise and chaos but it was one he relished – for the most part. That being said, he still did appreciate the quieter times when the kids were off on holidays with their grandparents when it had been just him and Liam all alone again.

They had also seen the world together, even living in Europe for nearly fifteen years when the children were growing up, as they'd wanted to expose them to as much history and culture as possible. Based in London, they'd often taken the kids away for weekend to nearby countries. During their time there, all three of their children learned to speak at least one other language fluently – with a smattering of several others – and at a much faster rate than their parents, Oscar in particular. It wasn't altogether surprising given the sponge-like learning capabilities of children's brains.

I wish my parents had done the same for me.

While Oscar struggled, Liam proved to have a knack for it, with the foreign words and phrases dripping off of his tongue much more easily. That being said, Oscar was content to be able to get by in exotic locales without coming across as the typical rude tourist demanding that the locals speak 'American'. Unfortunately, they had encountered more than a few of that ilk in their travels. Nonetheless, Oscar had still managed to unintentionally insult a few people along the way. Like the time he'd tried to order a certain pasta dish at a Sicilian restaurant and somehow insinuated that the owner's mother was less than virtuous when it came to the neighborhood men. Fortunately, an outrageously generous tip had smoothed things over.

The family had enjoyed their time abroad so much that at one point, it looked as if they would stay there indefinitely. This changed, however, when returning from the beach one summery afternoon in Barcelona, Oscar received some unsettling news regarding his father, Victor.

"Dad's had a heart attack!" bemoaned Oscar, upon listening to a voice mail.

"Oh dear! Is he OK?" asked Liam, great concern in his voice.

"Yeah, Mom said he was stable and not to worry. But how can I not?"

"Do you want to go home?"

"Yes. Even if he is OK now, I'd never forgive myself if he'd died before we could see him."

"Of course. I'll book the tickets now."

"Thank you. I'll go tell the kids." Oscar went to leave but stopped in his tracks and turned back to face his husband. "But I was just wondering…"

"Yes?"

"What if we moved back to the States?"

"Permanently?"

"Yes, well for a while at least. I mean none of our parents are getting any younger."

The pair had broached the topic before but it'd had never gone past gentle musings. Now, of course, the stakes were higher. Liam walked close to Oscar and brought him in a tender embrace.

"I don't care where we live as long as we're together."

Oscar immediately felt lighter but was then hit by a wave of doubt.

"What about the kids? They love it over here. I don't want to disrupt their lives. We already did it once when we moved over here in the first place."

"There's nothing to stop them coming back when they're older," reasoned Liam. "Besides they've already seen much more of the world than many of their friends back home."

"Thank you for always knowing just what to say."

"It's a gift," declared Liam smugly. "And my parents aren't spring chickens either."

Reassured, Oscar returned to his task of informing his offspring of their imminent travel plans. Naturally, there had been a spot of teenage angst and disgruntled complaining but within a year they were all happily living back in Port Davinica. Thankfully, both sets of grandparents ended up spending quite a few years more on the mortal coil but Oscar didn't doubt they'd made the right choice in coming home.

* * *

As expected, with all his reminiscing about married life, Oscar couldn't help but to remember the times where it hadn't quite been plain sailing. They had fought from time to time; as most couples are want to do, although usually just minor squabbles that barely lasted a few hours with only the faint touch of light-hearted resentment lingering afterwards.

Though there was one period, when it seemed like they might not make it to their next anniversary. It was about a year after they'd returned to the States and their home life had become a tad stressful. They had three teenagers at home, all of whom were testing their parents' patience at different times, by missing curfews, exploding in tears and generally providing a good deal of torment. On top of this, while Oscar's dance classes were full of eager students, Liam's new business, a secondhand bookstore called A Likely Story, wasn't doing so well. The first few months had seen an influx of enthusiastic shoppers but the numbers had steadily dwindled causing a dent in their savings and increased tension between the couple.

After the third big row in as many weeks, it was obvious that something needed to be done and Oscar had just the thing.

"A week in New York, just by ourselves. We could go next month during Gay Pride," declared Oscar. "What do you think?"

"OK, but what about the kids?" countered Liam a tad grumpily.

"My parents have agreed to come and watch the angst-fueled monsters, leaving us free to actually have some fun for a bit. Come on we both *need* this."

"Well, we haven't really partied since Europe." A sly smile graced Liam's lips, as the possibilities obviously played through his mind. "Sounds like fun. Let's do it!"

The break got off to a good start and without the pressure of their everyday family life the guys were able to relax; in fact, they hadn't bickered at all since they'd left Port Davinica. After a week spent playing tourist and remembering how nice a teenager-free existence could be, they decided to end their trip with a bang and spend the weekend on Fire Island. Fortune smiled upon the couple and they were able to find last minute accommodation with a friend of a friend, who lived in a pleasant house with a large pool and strolling distance to The Pines Beach. On the Saturday afternoon, their lodgings also happened to be the venue for a private pool party that was packed with gentlemen of a certain persuasion sporting an array of colorful, if somewhat skimpy, swimwear. Not wanting to stand out for all the wrong reasons, Oscar and Liam had also donned swimmers that didn't conceal a great deal and garnered a good deal of attention. It no doubt helped that they were both in fantastic shape despite the rigors of family life. Standing by the edge of the pool, the lads were about to take another dip when an old acquaintance made an unexpected reappearance into their lives.

"I'd recognize those asses anywhere!" declared a deep, gruff voice from behind them.

Turning around, Oscar and Liam were presented with the familiar sight of Darren Kennedy. Even in his early fifties he was still a handsome gent with midnight black hair, crystal blue eyes and a pale complexion. He was clad only in a pair of scandalously small electric-blue Speedos that did very little to hide the nine inches of thick uncut manhood between his legs – something the lads had had the pleasure of playing with in the past.

They'd first encountered Darren a good decade beforehand, coincidentally at another pool party, which had culminated in a very enjoyable threesome together. Since then, there'd been several more similarly fun catch-ups but they'd eventually lost touch when Darren had moved to Australia for work. Darren was hardly the first man to share their bed over the course of their relationship – their marriage being open and closed at different points – but it had been a little while since the last.

"They'll invite anyone to these things," joked Oscar.

"I *met* the owner last year in Mykonos," replied Darren with a suggestive smirk.

"Must've been a fun meeting," remarked Liam, grinning.

"I'm glad I ran into you guys. I've just moved back into your neck of the woods and didn't know how to get in touch with you."

Oscar exchanged a mischievous look with his husband, fairly certain that Liam was thinking the exact same thing.

Looks like this holiday is going to be even better for stress relief than I thought.

"Well we're here to touch now." Oscar brazenly tweaked Darren's dark brown nipple.

"Among other things," added Liam as he tweaked the other nipple.

"Sounds like a plan to me" agreed Darren, slapping both of them playfully on the butt.

The trio enjoyed an amiable afternoon frolicking in the water, getting tipsy on delightfully strong cocktails and becoming increasingly handsy with one another. As the sun began to set, their inhibitions were long gone and they were openly making out and rigorously groping one another – much to amusement of the other partiers, many of who were engaged in similar behavior.

"Shall we continue this upstairs?" suggested Oscar.

"Lead the way, good Sir," said Darren.

The intoxicated and extremely horny men proceeded upstairs where their swimwear was soon flung off and they fell into a messy tangle of limbs. Happily, the sex was even better than Oscar had remembered – more experience always helps.

Over the rest of the weekend they enjoyed each other's company repeatedly and were sore but sated come the time to return home. They exchanged details and promised to stay in touch.

"Don't be strangers, now" laughed Darren, giving each of the couple a hearty goodbye kiss.

Returning home, the couple enjoyed a renaissance of their relationship. The week spent away having reinvigorated their ardor for one another. Of course, this passion occasionally spilled over into trysts with Darren, who became a semi-regular addition to their playtime, as well as a close friend.

Sadly, their relationship was again threatened a mere six months later when a freak electrical storm caused a fire at A Likely Story and burnt it to the ground. In a cruel twist of fate, the bookstore had only recently begun to turn a profit again. Unsurprisingly, the insurance company dragged their heels in processing the claim and that coupled with the pressures of daily life once again began to take their toll. The couple's bickering soon reached the point where they were no longer having sex and could barely be in one another's company for longer than ten minutes before they'd start sniping at one another.

"Maybe we should take a break?" suggested Liam after yet another squabble.

"You want to leave me?" demanded Oscar angrily.

"No! But I can't keep on going like this."

Yeah, like I'm having a blast.

"This is marriage." Oscar's words were full of resentment. "Sometimes it's hard work."

"I don't want to break up the family but I just need to work out what I want."

"What about the kids? What the fuck are we going to tell them?"

"They're old enough to understand and it's hardly like they haven't noticed us fighting. It's probably better for them too."

He can't leave us. He can't leave me.

"Please don't do this!"

"I need some space dammit!" yelled Liam, clearly at the end of his tether. "I need to work out what I want to do. Find my way forward."

Realizing that there was no use fighting further, Oscar swung into a mode of sour resignation.

"Fine. You take all the damn space you need. Just don't expect me to wait around here forever!"

"I'll be at Darren's."

"What a surprise!" Venom dripped from Oscar's words. "Don't choke on his cock while you're *finding* yourself."

"I can't talk to you when you're like this!"

And with that Liam stormed out. He'd returned the following day to pick up some clothes.

The next few weeks were the most miserable that Oscar had ever spent. He and Liam were civil in their communication but the distance hadn't appeared to do anything to resolve their problems. Things may have gone on like this indefinitely if providence hadn't intervened.

It was a snowy December night when Oscar received a phone call that every parent dreads.

"I'm sorry to inform you Mr. Nightingale but your daughter Ella has been in a car accident," stated the authoritative voice of Constable Davis.

"Oh my god! Is she OK?" Oscar gripped the phone so tightly his knuckles turned white and his voice was trembling. "What happened?"

"Now, she's alright and just a little shaken up. It appears that she and her friends had been drinking at a party when they decided to drive home and ended up crashing. Fortunately, there were no fatalities…apart from the car and the tree it crashed into. In fact, the occupants got off lightly considering their stupidity."

"Where is she? Can I see her?"

"Yes, of course. You can come collect her from Sacred Heart Hospital."

"I'll be there shortly."

Jumping in the car, Oscar called Liam and picked him up on route, all their problems set aside in the concern for their daughter. After entering the Emergency Room they soon found their sixteen-year-old daughter, in the waiting area looking ashen and decidedly repentant.

"Please don't be mad," Ella tearily begged her parents.

"Of course not, princess," reassured Oscar, hugging her tight.

"We're just so glad you're safe," added Liam.

In that moment, all the animosity between the pair vanished, their only focus on their daughter.

"Are you OK? Have you seen the Doctor?" asked Oscar gently.

"Yes, but I need to go to the police station tomorrow to give my statement." Ella replied shamefaced. "I'm so, so sorry."

"We can deal with that later. For now, let's just get you home."

"Are you coming too, Daddy?" she asked turning towards Liam.

Liam looked to Oscar with pleading eyes in an unspoken question.

"Of course, pumpkin," answered Oscar. "He wouldn't go anywhere else."

Naturally, things weren't completely healed between Liam and Oscar but the accident gave them the push they needed to salvage their marriage. They agreed to counseling and over the course of a good many therapy sessions they managed to repair the fractures in their relationship. It helped that their love was still unquestionably strong, even though their petty gripes towards one another had made that harder to remember. To help, their marital bed was once more closed to outsiders, although Darren remained one of their dear friends.

In the end, their relationship became stronger for it. Not to say they never had any other problems but their arguments were talked out and they never again took the drastic step of separation…not voluntarily.

Several years later, on their thirtieth anniversary, Oscar and Liam renewed their vows with all the children and grandchildren in attendance. It was a most happy day for all concerned. The remembrance caused Oscar to become a touch misty eyed.

I'd marry him again and again and again…

* * *

After the last of the speeches, Oscar watched with enormous pride as Lachlan led Mackenzie onto the dance floor for their first official dance together. There were a great many flashes, as the assembled guests appeared to be in heavy competition with the official photographer – everyone eagerly trying to record the moment for posterity.

Turning towards Liam, Oscar could see his feelings reflected in the face of his husband, who was smiling widely at the newlyweds.

Life is such a wonderful thing.

Watching them glide about the dance floor, it took Oscar back to his own first dance as a married man and, of course, the wedding night. Drunk on champagne, the pair had stumbled upstairs to their oceanfront honeymoon suite. Sloppily kissing as they entered the room, the alcohol had only increased their ardor.

"Hot tub?" suggested Liam, mischief written all over his face.

"You read my mind."

Stripping out of their suits, the lads made their way naked out on to the balcony. Liam grabbed a bottle of complementary champagne from the fridge and two glasses, while Oscar switched on the hot tub, turning the still water into an inviting, steamy cauldron. The balcony looked out over the blackness of the water and gave an unobstructed view of the twinkling stars up above.

Once seated, they clinked their champagne flutes together for what seemed like the millionth toast of the day.

"To my dashing husband," toasted Oscar.

"To my handsome spouse," added Liam. "And the sexiest teacher I ever had."

"You got that right."

"Except for Mr. Lopez, my high-school Spanish teacher, he was pretty damn…"

Oscar silenced his cheeky husband with a voracious kiss. Putting their respective glasses to the side, the pair continued to lovingly kiss and caress one another, sliding their bodies together and enjoying the agreeable sensation of the hot water bubbling around them. After looking forward to that moment the whole day, Oscar fully intended on taking his time.

In spite of the heavy alcohol consumption, their manhoods rose to the occasion, albeit a tad more slowly than normal. When Oscar felt Liam's erection return to full force he slid fully onto his husband's lap. Using his right hand, Oscar then grasped the manhood and guided it into its home. Relaxed from the hot water, and the champagne, his opening yielded easily and he soon felt all of the wonderfully thick inches as they opened up his passage and filled him comfortably. When his buttocks touched down against Liam's hips, Oscar contracted his ass muscles, squeezing the member inside and causing Liam to groan. Leaning his face forward, Oscar gently kissed his husband's soft, full lips. Unhurriedly, he began to lift himself up and down, riding Liam's cock, milking it with his passage as he gazed deep into his husband's kind brown eyes.

As they played, Liam ran his hands all over Oscar, the edges of his fingernails leaving faint pink lines in their wake as they scratched against the slick skin. They continued on like this quite some time, consummating their marriage through deliciously slow lovemaking. It was hardly the first time they'd had such gentle sex but it would be fair to say it was among the most tender of their experiences.

After a while, Oscar was overcome with a desire to take his husband in return, so he lifted himself up off of the solid member and stood in the water. Grabbing Liam in his arms, Oscar spun him around so that he was bent over the edge of the hot tub looking outwards to the ocean. The sight of Liam's glistening defined back, and the pert ass at its base, caused Oscar's cock to grow even harder in anticipation. Receiving no objection from Liam – not likely given his versatile tendencies – Oscar placed his cockhead between Liam's firm, round cheeks and began to push into the tight entrance. As the velvet heat encased his manhood, Oscar let out a small sigh of satisfaction.

His strokes may have started softy but with encouragement from Liam, Oscar was soon hammering away into his husband's firm buttocks. The water splashed around them and onto the wooden deck of the terrace, as their movements became more frenzied. The intensity of his thrusts had their desired effect and Oscar grunted as he climaxed and spurted his load deep inside the welcoming tunnel.

Pulling out, Oscar then turned Liam around, gave him a fiery kiss and lifted him up onto the side. Diving forward he took Liam's throbbing cock deep into his throat and with practiced ease brought his husband to a rousing orgasm less than a minute later. As the cock erupted into his mouth, Oscar began to swallow furiously, desperate to drink down all of the salty-sweet nectar. Once he'd sucked it dry, he moved his head back up and gave Liam yet another hungry kiss, dragging him back into the water, where they continued their play.

Happily, and not at all surprisingly, such scenes had continued all throughout their honeymoon. They'd carefully chosen to stay in a private bungalow, on a small tropical island frequented by like-minded gents. The majority of their days were spent soaking up the sun and pleasuring one another until their bodies were in desperate need of rest and recuperation. By the time they got home, it was a wonder their balls ever managed to become replenished given the number of times they'd been drained dry. Thankfully, there proved to be quite a deal of seed left when it came time to grow a family of their very own.

Damn that was a good trip.

* * *

Glancing across the table, Oscar noticed Liam lift his glasses and rub his eyes. It was a gesture that Oscar had seen countless times over the years and knew his husband was feeling sleepy and would undoubtedly toddle off to bed shortly. For his part, Oscar was still wide-awake. Indeed, he never seemed to tire these days and was content to preside over the rest of the reception.

I think I'll stay a bit longer. It's nice to see everyone so happy.

Just as Oscar predicted, Liam left a few minutes later after saying his goodbyes. Oscar watched him go with a touch of regret. They had been separated for almost six months now and he desperately missed being with his husband. It hadn't, however, been a mutual decision. In fact, it was the very last thing Oscar wanted and the same could be said for Liam. Sadly, there are some things that are unavoidable – Oscar's death being one of them.

It had all come as a bit of a shock that first morning when Oscar was woken by Liam calling his name and loudly sobbing.

"Oscar! Dear god no, not yet!" begged Liam. "Please wake up!"

Confused, Oscar sat up and tried to calm his beloved down.

"Liam? What's wrong? What's going on?"

It was only when his hand sailed straight through his husband that Oscar grasped the gravity of his predicament. Bounding from the bed with an agility he hadn't possessed for years, Oscar was confronted with the most disturbing sight of his own lifeless body and his husband in an awfully desperate state beside it. The sobering realization of his death came quickly, followed in short order by a barrage of other thoughts.

Isn't there supposed to be a bright white light? Am I in heaven? Hell? Surely this can't be all there is. What on earth do I do now?

Over the following weeks, Oscar stayed close to his grieving family, extremely dismayed that he couldn't comfort them in their time of need. It was decidedly odd to attend his own funeral, albeit in incorporeal form, and he couldn't help but wonder if his previously departed friends had also been hanging about after their demises. Admittedly, it did please Oscar that the service was very well attended with a good many tearful, heartfelt speech.

Didn't think I was that popular!

In a strange way, Oscar was also content to see that his friends and family were enjoying themselves at his wake – although he had instructed for there to be such behavior in his will. Understandably, Liam looked thoroughly miserable but it gave Oscar solace to see his husband being consoled by their nearest and dearest.

At least there was one pleasant side effect of his mortally-challenged condition – Oscar could still communicate with the living in their dreams. So, over the past months he'd often entered the minds of his husband and family in their sleep and did his best to try and ease their pain. Naturally, the dreams with Liam had taken on a rather sexual note, taking them back to the peak of their sex life and beyond.

Who knew I was so flexible?

In his afterlife, Oscar occasionally encountered other ghosts but for the most part they were more focused on their own unfinished business that was keeping them in this realm. Without question, Oscar knew what was stopping him from moving on – Liam. Oscar was determined to hang around for as long as it took for him to be sure that his grieving husband would be all right. After all, he had nowhere else pressing to be.

I'd wait an eternity for him.

* * *

Some hours later, after his granddaughter and her new husband had made their departure and the guests slowly drifted away, Oscar also made a move to leave.

It really was a wonderful day, but I should go check on Liam.

He floated towards the doors and was about to exit through them when he was stopped dead by a most unexpected sight.

It can't be!

"Liam?"

"Oscar?" asked the apparition in the doorway. "Is that you? You look so young!"

"So do you, my love."

Rushing forward Oscar took Liam into his arms, and into a passionate embrace. Their ghostly forms, while mostly insubstantial to the mortal world, were solid enough when in contact with one another.

"I'm not dreaming?" Liam questioned in a disbelieving tone. "I really am dead?"

"I'm afraid so, my dear." Oscar gently took Liam's hands in his. "I wish I could say that I'm sorry but I'm so glad to be with you properly again."

"Me too!"

Reunited in death, Oscar couldn't have been happier… until he remembered where they were.

"Oh dear. Poor Mackenzie. She'll be heartbroken."

"Oh, I hadn't even thought," said Liam, his voice tinged with remorse. "How awful for it to happen on her wedding day."

"I wouldn't worry too much about Mackenzie though, she's a tough cookie. Gets that from her Poppy." Oscar squeezed Liam's arm affectionately. "And she has Lachlan and the rest of the family to lean on."

"I guess; it's just such a shame." His downtrodden look was then quickly replaced with a much happier regard. "But at least we're together again."

"Yes, there's that. Come here, Mister."

Pulling Liam towards him, Oscar embraced his husband, this time for a much longer and ardent coupling. Around them the last of the guests returned to their rooms and the staff finished clearing away, oblivious to the supernatural goings-on in their midst. The lights were dimmed, leaving the ghostly duo all alone in the semi-darkness.

"I've missed you so much!" gushed Liam.

"I know. I've been here. I'm just sorry that I couldn't comfort you more than in your dreams."

Liam's face lit up at the unexpected revelation.

"You naughty devil! I thought they all felt too realistic."

"What can I say?" remarked Oscar impishly. "I couldn't help myself."

"Well considering how…umm…*delightful* they were, I guess you're forgiven."

Oscar held Liam close, breathing his scent in deeply, half-afraid that it wasn't real. He'd been longing for Liam to join him but hadn't dared hope it would be so soon.

"So, what now?" demanded Liam, curiosity burning in his eyes. "Do we go somewhere? Are there angels waiting? What do we do? Are there some sort some of rules?"

That's my Liam.

"Always so inquisitive and practical…and impatient!"

"I'm sorry, it's just all a little overwhelming. It wasn't how I planned to end my day. It was a beautiful wedding though, wasn't it?"

"That it was." Offering up his hand, Oscar asked. "May I have this dance?"

"It would be my pleasure, kind Sir."

As they glided to the dance floor, familiar music began to softly play.

"Is that our song?" asked Liam, his eyes wide with wonder.

"Yeah, another *perk* of the afterlife."

Spinning onto the dance floor, they held their tight embrace, as they moved in time to a song that they'd danced to many times over the last sixty years. Swirling around the polished floorboards, Oscar gazed deeply into his beloved's beautiful chocolate-brown eyes. At the far end of the room a small, white light appeared. Barely noticeable at first, it soon grew in size and intensity until the whole room was bathed in its pure brightness.

"Time to go?" asked Liam.

"I think it might be." Oscar was filled with an almost overwhelming sense of happiness. "I'd go anywhere with you, my love."

The twosome continued to dance as the whiteness surrounded and enveloped them. Their bodies soon became mere shadows and then disappeared completely; the lovers making that final stop on their journey together.

THE PREACHER'S SON

Asher Richards was presently caught in a bit of a quandary. Well, to be honest, it was actually more of a hellish nightmare from which there appeared to be no escape. Not only was he locked in a furious battle with his stomach to avoid the almost overwhelming urge to throw up, but he was also on the verge of bursting into an unstoppable torrent of tears. Ideally, he would've loved to simply turn on his heel and run screaming down the aisle of the church, fly through the heavy wooden doors at the entrance and disappear off into the distance. Failing that, the ground opening beneath him and swallowing him whole would suffice. Indeed, he would have preferred almost anything at all than having to stand there and watch the love of his life get married to someone else.

Even though the day was pleasantly warm, his fitted black suit felt itchy and uncomfortable. As a result, he'd begun to fidget irritably. To his left stood Jeremiah Wilson, Asher's best friend and newlywed-to-be. He was a strapping young man with chestnut brown curls, clear blue eyes and a smile that melted Asher's heart on a daily basis. Asher loved Jeremiah more than he'd ever loved anything and that was why he'd agreed to be his best man, no matter how much he desperately didn't want to be and completely against his better judgment. To make matters worse, Asher's father, Preacher Henry Richards, was conducting the ceremony.

This day couldn't possibly be any more messed up. I wish it was done and I could move on with my life. Why must God punish me so?

The church for the ceremony, St Peters, was well over one hundred years old and was situated smack bang in the centre of Magnolia Falls – so named for the large number of Magnolia trees about the place and the picturesque waterfalls nearby. Despite being rather modest in design, with bare wooden floorboards and simple benches, the church did feature a magnificent stained glass window behind the altar, through which poured the sunshine of the late spring day. Behind the church was a fragrant rose garden, which was where the wedding photographs were scheduled to take place – practically a tradition for all the freshly married couples of the area.

Trying to keep calm, Asher looked at his best friend's profile, the big Roman nose heralding the size of other body parts that Asher knew oh so well.

No, I can't think about that. Not now, not ever.

Brushing those forbidden thoughts aside, Asher tried to keep his face impassive lest it betray the maelstrom of emotion swirling within his chest. As the Preacher began the service, Asher's mind flitted back over the years and he soon became lost in his thoughts about how he had come to this heartbreaking juncture and what was to become of him now.

I can't believe it's all gone so wrong.

* * *

Magnolia Falls was a close-knit community where everyone knew everyone else – and everyone else's business. Not to say that a few secrets hadn't slipped under the radar of the town gossips from time to time. For instance, no one knew that the former librarian, old Mrs. Hargreaves had had a torrid affair with a fellow librarian that lasted over several years at successive state conferences, or that the burly butcher, Mr. Fingus, enjoyed wearing his wife's panties when she was out of town visiting her sister – she was a larger woman so there'd been no telltale signs of stretching. And, of course, no one had discovered that Asher and Jeremiah were desperately in love with one another.

They had been steadfast companions for as long as Asher could remember. In fact, they'd known each other their whole lives, having been born less than a month apart. Their respective parents had always been on good terms and encouraged the friendship, as neither of the boys had a biological brother to roughhouse with. Even when they weren't together, Asher had a constant reminder of his best friend in the form of an old arrowhead, attached to a thin, brown leather strap that he wore around his neck. It was a cherished possession that Jeremiah had given to Asher for his tenth birthday and he'd never taken it off since.

While both were relatively popular lads growing up, with no shortage of other eager playmates, more often than not the pair could be found spending time by themselves. They had even built a secret tree house together near the small lake at the back of the Wilson's property, where it bordered with the Gambetta National Park. There had also been many hours spent chasing one another through the cornfields of the Wilson's farm, accompanied by Jeremiah's faithful golden retriever, Sunshine, who'd energetically run after them. Sadly, he'd gone to the great doggy heaven just after they'd graduated high school.

Asher found everything about Jeremiah endearing, even his best friend's childhood stutter, which had drawn the ire of bullies. The cruel taunting had only stopped after Asher stood up against the ringleader, Todd Finkle, and given him a rather impressive black eye. For his trouble, Asher had received Jeremiah's even greater devotion and several lashes of his father's belt – the Preacher was ever the disciplinarian.

It was worth it.

It wasn't until their late teenage years that the relationship between them changed and a growing mutual attraction had made itself known. It had all started innocently enough with a spot of evaluation, where they had compared the size of their respective manhoods – Jeremiah's was a tad longer at eight-and-a-half inches but Asher possessed a thicker girth. Naturally, this had progressed to jacking off in front of one another, followed several sessions later with mutual masturbation. Both lads were uncut and they very much enjoyed playing with each other's foreskins, stretching and teasing them to great delight.

The turning point from curiously messing about to something more serious, however, had come with their first kiss. They had been pleasuring each other for a few weeks, when Jeremiah did something completely unexpected. Instead of the usual routine of quickly cleaning up, pulling up their pants and getting back to whatever they'd been doing beforehand – in this case, exploring the woods around their tree house – Jeremiah moved forward and brushed his lips over Asher's, pressing gently with just the barest hint of tongue.

A little shocked, Asher moaned lightly as the kiss sent an electric thrill from his mouth down through his body and back up again.

"Was that, OK?" asked Jeremiah tentatively.

The kiss awakened in Asher a longing that he'd been suppressing; scared it could ruin their friendship. He knew then and there what he truly wanted and needed.

"Yeah, more than OK. Come here."

Pulling Jeremiah to him, Asher returned the kiss with interest; their tongues soon began hungrily exploring each other's mouths as their nubile bodies pulled in snugly together. From that point, their sessions always involved a great deal of kissing before, during and after, their reciprocal handiwork. Over the following weeks, their play became more exploratory, leading into fellatio and some light fingering. Even so, it was then some months before they had properly lost their virginity to one another.

The fateful day fell on Asher's birthday, the summer after high school graduation, and Jeremiah had texted Asher to meet him in the small barn at the far end of his family farm that they used to store surplus materials – one of their many play spots.

Jeremiah: *Hurry up, birthday boy! I have a surprise for you.*

Asher: *Be there soon.*

After climbing the wooden ladder up to the landing where they usually messed about, Asher came upon the pleasing sight of Jeremiah laying on his back on a hay bale, buck naked with his legs spread wide in the air and a cheeky grin upon his face. If his intention wasn't obvious enough, then the open can of Crisco – secreted away from his mother's pantry and placed conveniently by his side – certainly left no doubt to what Jeremiah had in mind. Asher felt a rising in his heart and his crotch. To this day, the smell of hay always made Asher's manhood swell in remembrance.

"Happy Birthday, Ash! Time to claim your present."

"Miah? Are you sure?"

"Damn sure! Don't you want it?"

In response, Asher ripped of his clothes and lay down on top of Jeremiah delivering a series of frantic kisses. After a few minutes, Asher dipped his fingers into the Crisco and scooped out a generous dollop of the thick grease, and proceeded to lubricate both his manhood and his best friend's rosebud.

Placing his cockhead at the entrance, Asher felt the inviting warmth emanating from the tunnel, which naturally excited him and caused his precum to moisten the area even more. As he pushed forward and began to enter the tight hole, his foreskin slipped back allowing his glans direct contact with the velvety walls. This raw connection felt almost as if their bodies were melting together.

This is awesome!

Jeremiah winced as he was first penetrated but his pained expression quickly turned into a satisfied grin, which delighted Asher as he sank in all the way to the hilt. He moved forward to kiss Jeremiah lovingly on the mouth, keeping his hips still and allowing his best friend to adjust to the invader inside.

Starting with small gentle movements, Asher carefully worked his erection in and out of the snug passageway. Emboldened by Jeremiah's increasingly loud moans, and led by his own unchecked desire, Asher's strokes grew longer and faster. Beads of sweat appeared on his forehead and trickled their way down his body as he merrily toiled away. The arrowhead swung on the necklace and bounced off of his chest as his hips increased in speed and he began to thrust away in earnest. The hay scratched against his legs as he pounded into Jeremiah's tight virgin passage – it provided a delightful contrast of pleasure and pain.

It wasn't too long before Jeremiah's groans turned more guttural as he obviously approached orgasm; a fact confirmed mere moments later as his manhood erupted, sending thick white ropes of manly seed over his heaving chest and abdominals. The subsequent clenching of Jeremiah's sphincter around Asher's member was enough to drive him fully over the edge as well, and he growled in pleasure as he unloaded deep inside his best friend.

Collapsing down on top of Jeremiah, Asher felt spent and elated. After a few moments Asher sat up a little, his heart was brimming with emotion and he urgently needed to pronounce the words that he'd uttered in his head a million times but hadn't yet been brave enough to say out loud.

"I love you, Miah."

Jeremiah looked straight back into his Asher's eyes, his face alight with joy at hearing those special words, and gave his own confession.

"I've loved you for forever."

After a short break to recover, Asher decided it was only fair to return the favor. He stood up, pulling Jeremiah to his feet and gave him a deep loving kiss before bending over the very same bale and offering himself to the man he loved.

Eagerly accepting the invitation, Jeremiah wasted no time lubing himself and Asher up and soon had his bulbous cockhead pressing against the inviting entrance.

Gasping as the mushroom-head breached his sphincter, Asher's discomfort soon faded into a pleasurably full sensation as Jeremiah's inches slowly stretched his insides. While Jeremiah started with a leisurely pace it soon became far more frenzied, with the sounds of skin slapping together, coupled with their manly sounds of enjoyment, echoing throughout the barn. Unsurprisingly, the fierce pumping brought about another round of ejaculations. Jeremiah's cream splashed into Asher heating his insides, while Asher's own seed spurted along his stomach and seeped down into the hay below him.

Since then they had taken every opportunity they could to fuck, careful not to rouse the suspicions of their families, who would be horrified if they'd learnt the truth about the nature of boys' relationship. They'd also learned to take their time, savoring each heavenly sensation in ever-lengthening sessions. That being said, the pair still enjoyed the occasional rough, quicker bouts of frantic play.

Over the years, they had explored every last part of each other's bodies. Indeed, there wasn't a square inch of Jeremiah that Asher didn't absolutely adore. Jeremiah's muscles had been honed to perfection from the manual labor he performed on the farm and the sun had bronzed his lightly haired skin a delicious golden honey brown. It was all so wonderfully different from Asher's own slighter build, smooth skin and much darker coloring. In particular, Asher loved the small, purplish port-wine stain birthmark on Jeremiah's left buttock, often running his fingers over it and licking it whenever he had the chance.

Often, after a bout of energetic lovemaking, the lads speculated on their future. Even though they knew it was unrealistic, it didn't stop the pair from wanting a life together. Both adored living in Magnolia Falls, but they also knew that their community could be somewhat closed-minded. Jeremiah dreamed of owning an apple orchard, where he could work the land and they could be free to spend the rest of their days together. It was a fantasy Asher shared and that frequently flitted through his daydreams.

If only.

* * *

Despite the fulfillment he received from being with Jeremiah, Asher had long begun to tire of leading a double life. To his family, and the town in general, he was the quiet librarian, who adored books and just hadn't met the right girl yet. The true version of himself only existed behind closed doors, where he was passionate young man in the midst of a steamy gay affair with his best friend.

Even with all his inner turmoil, Asher was fairly content with his job, having taken over the post three years previously when old Mrs. Hargreaves had taken ill and become bedridden. His passion for literature had actually been cultivated by his father's insistence on studying religious texts. From there Asher had well and truly fallen in love with the written word and eagerly read anything he could get his hands on. It came as no great surprise to anyone that he became the assistant librarian straight out of high school. Certainly, it seemed to be the perfect fit.

One advantage of his post, besides unlimited access to books, was that he was given free reign over ordering new titles, so had secreted away quite an array of exceedingly homoerotic books. In a more brazen display of rebellion, Asher and Jeremiah had taken to fucking amongst the religious folios after closing time on a semi-regular basis, although that was as far as their bravery had gone.

Around a month after he'd fully taken charge of the library, he'd had an opportunity to be completely honest with his family but Asher had been too afraid to take it. As a result, his younger cousin, Topher, had paid dearly for it, something that continued to be a source of great shame for Asher.

Arriving at his parents' place for their customary Friday dinner together, Asher found his mother, Maria, crying. She was a handsome woman in her early forties, with dark glossy hair, dark eyes and golden skin, which denoted her Hispanic origins, traits both Asher and his younger sister, Nina, shared. His father, Preacher Henry Richards, was a stout man in his mid-forties with prematurely grey hair, pale blue eyes and a ruddy complexion. He wore one of his famously dark looks upon his countenance.

"Mom, what's wrong. Is it Nina? Did something happen at her wilderness campout?"

"No, she's fine. It's…it's your cousin, Christopher."

"Topher? What happened?"

Before his mother could answer, Asher's father interrupted with his deep booming voice, his words full of self-righteous anger.

"Your aunt and uncle heard disturbing rumors about him. That he had…disgusting…unnatural thoughts. They confronted him and he didn't even attempt to deny it! He had the audacity to be proud of his filthy sinful urges! I don't know how such depravity reached Magnolia Falls, let alone our family. At least this moral rot has now been cut away and we can start to heal."

That's awful! He can't help it. It could've been me.

"Uncle Hank and Aunt Rosario kicked him out?" asked Asher, disbelief in his tone.

"And rightly so. He refused to repent for his wicked deviance, so they were left with no choice."

He's so young! How could they just disown him?

"But he's only fifteen where will he go?"

"If he refuses to return to the righteous path then he is already lost to us," thundered the Preacher. "You didn't know anything about this, did you, Asher?"

Struggling to keep his emotions in check, Asher felt sick to his stomach, his thoughts were laden with fear, guilt and ignominy.

Oh God! Do they suspect me too?

"No, of course not. How would I?"

"Well, you aren't that much older than him. You even used to play together when you were little."

"That was a long time ago," murmured Asher, his heart heavy. "We haven't really talked for ages."

Maybe if I kept closer to him, we could have helped each other through this.

"Leave the boy alone, Henry. He would have told us if he knew." Asher's mother looked towards him with pride in her eyes. "We brought him up in a decent manner. Isn't that right, Asher?"

"Yes, Ma'am." Surreptitiously glancing down at his watch, Asher had a sudden thought. "When did this happen?"

"An hour ago," answered his mother. "I only just got off the phone to your aunt."

I should go to the bus station; it's where I would've gone. The last bus out of town doesn't leave for another half hour. He's probably still there. I could help him. I should help him. But how can I leave without them getting suspicious?

"I'm…actually not feeling hungry, now. I…"

"Understandable son, it turns my stomach as well," stated the Preacher, the disdain clear on his face. "We need to pray together."

"But, I…"

"What? You don't think we should pray for our family in this dire time?"

"Please, Asher," pleaded his mother. "We need to seek the Lord's guidance."

"Yes, of course."

Reluctantly, Asher joined his parents in prayer, kneeling on the living room floor for a good half hour. This was followed by an uncomfortable dinner where Asher's father, in full preacher mode, ranted and railed against the evils of modern life . After the dinner, Asher bid goodbye to parents and then drove directly to the bus station in the vain hope of finding his cousin. Unsurprisingly, it was deserted, but he'd still driven around town for nearly an hour before acknowledging that Topher was undoubtedly long gone.

Feeling defeated, Asher texted Jeremiah and the pair soon met up at their spot in the old barn. As soon as Jeremiah arrived, Asher recounted the entire sorry story, his eyes wet with tears at the end of the telling.

"We can never come out to our families," lamented Asher. "And we can never really be together."

"You don't know that. Things could be different for us. We're adults, we can stand up to them."

"I want to believe that but…the look in their eyes when they were talking about Topher and how he was going to burn in hell for an eternity for his evil, unnatural ways. How can we possibly fight against that kind of ignorance?"

"I…I…I don't know."

"And I should've tried to help Topher. He's out there all alone and I've no way to help him or tell him that I understand."

"It's not your fault," reassured Jeremiah, bringing Asher into his strong arms. "You didn't make his parents behave so despicably. I know this sucks, but we'll get through this together and it'll be OK."

Not for Topher it won't.

Despite Jeremiah's warm embrace and encouraging words, the fear of rejection stabbed at his heart and the self-recrimination instilled into Asher by his father's sermons over the years weighed heavily on him.

The thought of losing his family and everything he'd known sent Asher into a sort of emotional paralysis, which in turn led to a temporary cooling of his relationship with Jeremiah. He even made excuses to stop seeing his best friend, feeling unworthy of the pleasure it brought.

I don't deserve this happiness. I abandoned Topher in his time of need, what sort of man am I?

Eventually, his love and longing for Jeremiah was too much to resist and Asher soon found himself back in his lover's arms. After what had happened with his cousin, the couple decided to make extra sure that no one suspected what they were really up to. To this end, they occasionally dated a few of the local lasses but it always fizzled out when things got too serious. Thankfully, their religious upbringing, and the forbidding of premarital relations, aided them in hiding their lack of attraction to the fairer sex. Fortunately, they didn't apply such notions to their own sex life, which continued to thrive in secret.

While the savage treatment of his cousin had first scared him into keeping quiet about his own proclivities, Asher's questioning of his strict religious upbringing only continued to grow.

How could a caring God want people to be cast out just for loving someone? Not my kind of God.

* * *

Regrettably, it was only a matter of time before the real world would once again intrude upon their happy bubble of secret happiness and send them towards the unpleasant future they were presently facing.

Around six months before the dreaded wedding day, the twosome met with a nasty shock when Jeremiah appeared to be on the verge of turning his dream of owning an orchard into a reality. His grandfather had already willed him a decent parcel of land, two years prior, but he still required a bit of capital to transform it into a viable orchard. Jeremiah had managed to save about half the money needed and his parents were prepared to help out financially, but only on the proviso of him being legally wed. It went without saying that they meant to a woman – though the laws had changed, his parents' prejudices had not. Jeremiah had been close to tears when they'd met up later that evening. He was so distraught that his childhood speech impediment made an unwanted return.

"Th...th...they said I'm n...no...not getting any younger and th...th...they w...want m...mo...more grandchildren.

Th…th…th…they want me to m…ma… marry Agnes Peterson!"

At the moment, Asher hated Agnes with a furious, blind passion. Even though he knew it wasn't her fault – in fact, he rather liked her – the rage inside Asher was toxic. She was a pleasant enough girl, a buxom blonde, a few years younger than them with friendly hazel eyes and child-rearing hips.

"Miah, I don't know what to say." Asher felt the beginnings of hot tears stinging his eyes. "What are we going to do?"

"Th…there's n…nothing w…we can do."

Apparently, his parents thought that at the ripe old age of twenty-five, Jeremiah needed help to continue the family line, seeing as he hadn't yet found a suitable woman to wed – or even appeared overly interested in doing so. His younger sister, Sandra, a delicate featured lass with bright auburn hair and clear blue eyes, was already married with two children and a third on the way.

The thought of losing Jeremiah filled Asher's heart with dread and he felt a wave of misery wash over him. Clinging to Jeremiah, Asher never wanted to let him go. He always feared this day would come and yet he was still completely unprepared to deal with the situation. All sorts of scenarios flitted through his mind, none of which had a happy outcome.

"If you w…wa…want m…me to, I…I'll give it all up and w…w…we can run away together."

Hope flitted through Asher's heart but it was almost immediately extinguished by an unwelcome voice of reason. Asher knew that if he wanted to maintain a good relationship with his family he could never tell them about his true desires and he also realized that he couldn't stand in the way of Jeremiah's dream.

We'd have to give up everything. Our families. The orchard. How can I take that away from him? He'd only end up resenting me. I love him too much for that to happen.

"No, we can't." Asher's voice was burdened with a sad resignation. "If you want the orchard, you have to marry her."

"I...I don't w...wa...want to lose you."

"I'll always be here for you." The next words sickened him and he barely got them out. "But we won't be together in the same way."

"I...I...I can't give you up."

Oh, God. This is so hard. I need to do what's best for him.

"You must. It's for the best."

They stood holding each other, neither wanting to let go. After a few minutes, Jeremiah stepped back slightly and looked at Asher with an uneasy expression.

"I...if I do th...this. I...I have to ask you something."

"Sure. Anything you need."

"W...wi...will you be my best m...man?"

NO! He can't expect that of me!

Angrily pushing Jeremiah away from him, Asher was absolutely shocked and appalled.

"Miah! How could you possibly ask me that?"

"I…I…I don't w…want to, but people w…w…will know something's wrong if you're n…not."

He's right! But I don't care! How can I watch him do that? But how can I leave him to face it alone?

"OK, fine." Asher's voice had developed a flat emotionless tone, numbness having temporarily replaced his anger. "I'll do it, but I have to go now."

"Can't w…w…we talk m…more about it?" pleaded Jeremiah. "I…I ne…need you."

"I can't. Not tonight. I need time."

Leaving Jeremiah in the barn, Asher fled back to his apartment, tears rolling down his cheeks the entire way.

* * *

Over the next few weeks, the pair barely spent any time together – mostly due to Asher's reluctance to be alone with Jeremiah and the temptation it represented. Even when they did consummate their love, the shadow of their soon-to-be ended relationship was ever present in Asher's mind. Not wanting to ruin what little time they still had left together, Asher had avoided talking about their predicament but the incessant voices in his head soon began to affect him physically, his inner turmoil resulting in a recurring upset stomach and the possible beginnings of an ulcer.

Unable to keep quiet any longer, Asher decided to address the problem the next time they met in private.

Jeremiah had arrived at Asher's apartment, freshly-showered after a hard day of work on the farm and greeted his best friend with a hungry kiss.

"What's wrong?" asked Jeremiah, an anxiousness hovering about his features.

"We have to stop," replied Asher, his voice full of sadness. "It's not right. I feel sick with worry and guilt all the time. We shouldn't…we can't make love any more."

"But we have to," implored Jeremiah. "While we still can."

"Miah, we need to…"

The rest of his sentence was swallowed by Jeremiah's urgent kisses. After a brief feeble protest, Asher gave into his instincts and the twosome were soon rolling around naked together in Asher's king-sized bed.

Regardless of Asher's discomforted mind, they did continue to lie with one another for another week or so, albeit on a decreasingly frequent basis. After the engagement had been officially announced, however, their sex stopped completely. As much as Asher loved Jeremiah and desperately craved his touch, he couldn't bring himself to betray or tarnish the commitment that his best friend had made to Agnes – no matter how much he wanted to. The guilt over his lustful thoughts and the unfairness of the situation meant that Asher was pretty much miserable a majority of the time. While his stomach felt better since they'd stopped coupling, his heart had a constant ache.

This is my own private Hell. Maybe God is vengeful, after all.

His torment wasn't helped whenever he encountered Agnes and Jeremiah out and about together, an unfortunately frequent occurrence given the size of their hometown. Each time he saw them acting like a devoted couple, it tore at his heart and generated all manner of uncharitable thoughts towards Agnes.

She doesn't deserve him! How will he even be able to get it up for her? She won't be able to satisfy him the way I can.

The change in his relationship with Jeremiah hadn't gone unnoticed, which Asher discovered whilst having his regular mid-week lunch with his mother – they shared a much closer relationship than he did with the Preacher. It was a practice they'd started when he first moved out of home into his modest apartment attached to the library – another one of the perks of the job.

"Did you and Jeremiah have a fight?" asked Asher's mother, with a concerned countenance. "You never seem to see talk about him any more and I don't remember the last time I saw you two together."

If only you knew.

"Nope." Asher tried to keep the bitterness and hurt from his voice but there was still a lingering trace. "He's just busy with the farm and planning the orchard…and the wedding stuff."

Obviously misreading the situation, his mother offered some reassuring advice.

"Don't worry, you'll find a nice girl and settle down too. Then you'll both be on an even footing again. Try not to be jealous of his happiness."

But he's not happy and neither am I!

"It's not…" Asher caught himself before he revealed the secret he'd been keeping for so long. "Yeah, I guess so. Can we talk about something else, please?"

"Yes, of course, Ashy."

Pushing down his turbulent emotions, Asher swiftly changed the topic to much less painful matters.

"That new John Grisham novel you wanted arrived yesterday."

"Oh, wonderful! I've been looking forward to it."

The rest of the lunch passed uneventfully, as did the rest of the week, the only constant being Asher's despair. After managing to avoid talking to Jeremiah at the Sunday church service, Asher returned home and listlessly moved about his apartment, not in the mood to read or do anything really. A sudden knocking at the door caused him to start, it was unusual, as he didn't tend to get any Sunday visitors.

I wonder who on earth that can be?

Opening the door, Asher was perturbed to discover Jeremiah standing on his doorstep with a pleading look in his eyes.

"Ash, I'm sorry for coming by unannounced but I needed to see you."

"You saw me at church."

"That's not what I meant." He stood there awkwardly for a moment, obviously uncomfortable. "Please, can I come in?"

"Where's Agnes?" The acidity in Asher's voice was unmistakable. "Shouldn't you be with her?"

A look of great hurt contorted Jeremiah's handsome features, which in turn caused pain in Asher's heart. He didn't mean to be so nasty but his emotions were getting the best of him.

It's better to keep pushing him away now. It'll hurt less later…I hope.

"She's with her family. Please, Ash. I need to talk to you. You won't answer my texts or calls and my family has been asking what's happened between us. Can't we just talk?"

Asher was reluctant to be alone with his best friend, worried that he wouldn't be able to control his natural impulses. That being said, he could see the anguish clearly etched on Jeremiah's face.

"OK, fine," agreed Asher with a sigh. "Come in."

"Thanks."

After ushering his best friend into his small, yet comfortable, living room, Asher turned to Jeremiah.

"Do you want something to drink?"

"There's only one thing I want."

Jeremiah closed the short distance between them and grasped Asher into a tight embrace, sealing their lips together. Asher struggled briefly against Jeremiah's advances but it was futile to resist. Giving into their carnal longings, the twosome was soon bare ass naked with Asher's cock buried deep inside the familiar embrace of Jeremiah's welcoming passage right there in the hallway – the lads unable to make it to the bed. All the emotion of the past month was released in a fierce bout of animalistic passion. Indeed, any passerby who'd heard their grunts and groans could be forgiven for thinking that they'd stumbled upon a pair of fighting wildebeests. Fortunately, the library was located off to the far end of the business district, which was often deserted of a weekend.

The steamy encounter was over rather quickly but left them both breathing heavily and their bodies slick with sweat. As they lay recovering from their exertions on the polished wooden floorboards of the hallway, Asher's mind was a jumble of conflicting thoughts.

This isn't right. But it feels so damn good. It can never happen again. I don't want to give him up...but I must.

Sitting up in a rush, Asher came to a firm decision.

"We can't keep doing this! You're getting married."

"Please, I need you so much," begged Jeremiah, as he moved to a seated position and took Asher's hand. "Just until the wedding. Otherwise I don't think I can go through with it. Please, Ash."

"It's not fair to ask that of me."

"I know and I'm sorry, but I'm desperate."

The beseeching look in his best friend's clear blue eyes yanked sharply at Asher's heartstrings and quickly put an end to his objections. Asher had never been particularly good at refusing Jeremiah, especially when it came to satisfying his manly needs. Although it wasn't just for Jeremiah's sake, as he too missed the affection and closeness they'd always shared.

"OK," agreed Asher with great misgivings. "Only until the wedding."

"Thank you so much!" gushed Jeremiah, pulling Asher in close to him. "You mean the world to me."

Apparently wanting to capitalize on the time they had left, Jeremiah recommenced kissing Asher and soon the pair was once more rolling around together in a happily writhing tangle of limbs.

This isn't a good idea. It's only for a few more months. This won't end well. God, he feels so good.

* * *

As the months to the wedding flew by at a disturbingly fast pace, Asher only became more despondent and upset at the prospect of losing Jeremiah permanently. Even though they were continuing to have sex clandestinely, the joy he felt at their coupling was constantly eroded by having to maintain the façade of simply being best friends. Rationally, Asher knew that it was a bad situation for them both, but there was a sense of resentment growing towards Jeremiah for placing him in this difficult position. His continuing unhappiness forced Asher to consider something he would never have thought possible – leaving Magnolia Falls for good.

Ever since agreeing to be there for Jeremiah, in the lead up to the wedding, Asher had been weighing his options. As much as the idea of leaving his beloved hometown was daunting and more than a little terrifying, Asher didn't really see a happy future for himself there. He was also conflicted, as apart from the overly conservative values, it was a lovely place to live. The air was clean, the townsfolk were generally friendly and the pace of life was pleasantly calm and relaxed. The idea of starting afresh in a new place wasn't particularly appealing but Asher knew that realistically if he was to move on from Jeremiah and have any chance of happiness with another like-minded gent, moving to a big city was his best option.

It'll be easier for both of us if we're not fully in each other's lives any more.

The thought of leaving his family behind, especially his mother and sister, was also a hard one to face. Begrudgingly, Asher realized that he'd even miss his father – in a way.

Once he'd come to the decision to leave, the question then was where to go. On that matter at least, he had one possible hope. About a year after Topher's parents had disowned their son, Asher had started searching for him. He had overheard from his own parents, mostly through the loud disgusted words of the Preacher, that Topher was living in Port Davinica – a large city quite a few hours to the north of Magnolia Falls – with a family who'd taken him in and adopted him as their own.

I'm so glad someone cared enough to help him. Better than I was.

After quite a bit of research online, Asher managed to track down Topher on social media, where he now went by the new surname of Walker. In the photos he could clearly see that his cousin appeared content with lots of new friends and a handsome boyfriend by his side.

I wish Jeremiah and I could be open and happy like that.

With great trepidation Asher had sent him a message on Facebook – after several drafts to get the wording just right – begging for forgiveness over his inaction and leaving his contact details. Nearly a week passed and Asher began to fear that he'd left his attempt of reconciliation far too late.

Would serve me right if he never wanted anything to do with me at all.

It was with great joy, however, when Asher turned on his phone one morning and discovered a text.

Unknown: *It's Topher. I forgive you. Call me. I'd like to talk.*

Despite the welcoming gesture, Asher still paced around his apartment for a good twenty minutes before he worked up the courage to call the number. His cousin answered on the third ring.

"Hi," said a familiar voice on the other end.

"Hi…it's Ash…Asher, your cousin."

"Yeah, I kinda knew that when your number flashed up."

"Oh, sorry, right." Asher was a bundle of nerves and barely knew where to begin, but then suddenly found a flood of words gushing out of him. "I just want to say that I'm sorry again for…for not standing up to your parents or mine. How they treated you was appalling and I should have done something. I acted cowardly and you deserved better from your family and from me. I don't know what God has planned for us, but I have to believe that he makes us exactly how he wants us and so how can anyone truly judge and condemn another person? It should be about love, not hate and I'm so sorry that I wasn't strong enough to be there for you."

There was a silence on the other end of the phone for about five seconds, which felt excruciatingly long to Asher and sent his mind whirling with unpleasant possibilities.

Oh, God. Why did I babble so much? He probably hates me even more.

"Wow, that was a lot."

"Umm, yeah…sorry."

"First off, you need to stop apologizing. I've made my peace with what happened and I don't blame you. Yes, I was disappointed when it felt like my whole family had turned against me but I know what it's like to grow up there. I don't know if I can ever forgive my…parents, but I've moved on and I have a new life…a better life."

"I can't tell you how happy that makes me." The relief was clear in Asher's voice. "I've been thinking about you a lot lately…and I hope we can be friends."

"I'm sure we can manage that."

They conversed amiably for another half hour or so with the promise to keep in touch, which they did. The pair began to regularly message and chat with one another and after two weeks Asher worked up the courage to confess the thing that no one besides Jeremiah knew.

"I'm…I'm gay too, and I've been having a secret relationship with Jeremiah Wilson for six years."

Somewhat dazed, Asher felt a great deal lighter after his admission. Moments later he was overcome with a strong sense of doubt and regret.

Maybe I shouldn't have told him. What have I done? Will he out us? That's not fair. He's given me no reason to think he'd be so vengeful.

"Wow…I definitely didn't see that coming," remarked Topher, his voice tinged with genuine surprise. "But, I totally understand. I always thought Jeremiah was ridiculously hot!"

"Yeah, me too." Asher gave a little laugh and felt his body relax, as his worst fears hadn't been realized and he now had a confidante. "And now you see why it was even more heinous of me for not stepping up and helping you when I had the chance."

Demonstrating a maturity beyond his years, Topher took the high road and instead of berating his cousin for past mistakes, he simply offered all the sympathy and support that Asher wished he'd given but had been too afraid to.

"I've told you before, I've already forgiven you. You're back in my life now and I'd like that to continue. I know how isolating it can be to live with that particular secret and all you can lose when it comes out, but to be honest I've never been happier and I think you can be too."

Their friendship only continued to grow over the next two years, although Asher didn't dare tell his family about their reconnection – keeping things hidden had become second nature by that point. Naturally, with the upcoming wedding and his dilemma over possibly leaving Magnolia Falls, Asher had turned to Topher for advice.

"I'm not sure that I'm doing the right thing," bemoaned Asher. "But I don't know how I can possibly stay here and not lose my mind."

"It would definitely be better for you to get away for a while," agreed Topher. "Why don't you come stay with me? There's more than enough room in my apartment."

"That's so generous of you but I just don't know."

"Trust me, I know how scary it is, but life is different here. It would be better if you and Jeremiah could leave together but if that's not possible, you should at least have the chance to escape and be happy, if that's still what you want to do."

"I'll think about it."

A week later, after Asher had given the matter a great deal of angst-ridden thought, he sent his cousin the message.

Ash: *I'm coming.*

* * *

The next two months passed by in a flash and to Asher's horror he found that it was only two more days to the wedding. He had agreed to spend one last night with Jeremiah before they would be forced to stop their intimate play forever. Of course, Jeremiah believed that it would only be the last time they had sex, not the last time he'd see Asher for a possibly rather long time.

I can't tell him. He'll be so hurt. Well, I'm hurting too. It's for the best.

In order to have the time alone, Jeremiah told his parents and friends that he really wanted to spend the day before wedding camping with his best friend, instead of a raucous bachelor party. Unsurprisingly, both sets of parents were pleased that the lads were choosing a more wholesome way to mark the occasion.

If they only knew.

Around mid-morning the pair headed off to their special spot in the woods by the small lake. Equipped with food and a good deal of alcohol, Asher tried to pretend that it was like it always had been and that their lives weren't about to change irrevocably.

I can't believe this is the end.

Brushing the unpleasant thoughts aside, Asher did his very best to enjoy their time together. Stretched out on the grassy bank between the tree house and the lake, they started in on their supply of beers and were soon reminiscing about their many, many happy past adventures. Around them the woods buzzed with life and the pleasant intermingled scents of wildflowers wafted around them. Given the unseasonable warmth of the spring day, it wasn't long before they decided to discard their clothes and splash about in their lake together, as they'd done countless times before. The sunshine beat down on their skin, making them glisten as they frolicked in the water. After a spot of almost carefree roughhousing, grasping at one another's slippery bodies and laughing, they came together and began to kiss. Tenderly at first, the intensity soon increased, as did the size of their manhoods, clearly broadcasting their arousal.

"Let's move to the side," suggested Jeremiah.

Happy to acquiesce, Asher let Jeremiah lead him back to the verdant bank of the lake. Lying down on his back, Jeremiah pulled Asher on top of him, where they continued their ravenous kissing. Their erections were pressed firmly together, oozing precum at a rapid rate, which then smeared between their writhing bodies

Several pleasurable minutes later, Asher began to kiss his way down Jeremiah's form, licking and biting the erect, dime-sized, brown nipples before descending further to the crotch. Grabbing a hold of the rigid member in his right hand, he used his mouth to pull the foreskin up over the swollen cockhead and proceeded to nibble on it in a practiced fashion. Exposing the glans again, Asher flicked his tongue back and forth over the sensitive cockhead, one of many moves he'd learnt that was always guaranteed to make Jeremiah squirm in delight.

Moving down further, Asher's lowered his head between Jeremiah's powerful thighs, lifting the muscular legs to expose the rosebud he knew so well. After appreciating the view for a moment, he shoved his face deep inside, his tongue penetrating the hole, surging and twirling about in a circular motion. He inhaled deeply, taking in the familiar musky scent and pushed his tongue in even further.

Satisfied that he'd thoroughly prepared the hole, Asher then spat on his hand and lined up his cockhead. Gazing deeply into Jeremiah's eyes, Asher pushed forward, carefully penetrated the tight ring and slowly slid inside, adoring the velvet heat that enveloped his manhood as it entered inch-by-inch. When he'd bottomed out, his balls resting against the plump buttocks, Asher moved forward to kiss Jeremiah and then began to make love to his best friend. Jeremiah's strong hands pulled at him, drawing him into an even tighter embrace. The gentle kissing soon became more insistent as Asher picked up the pace and hammered into him with ever-quickening strokes. His breathing became ragged as his orgasm edged closer to release. Less than a dozen quick thrusts later, Asher unleashed his cream with a grunt, spurting deep inside, all the while their mouths stayed connected, never breaking that intimate contact.

In no rush, the twosome stayed locked in this position, caressing one another and kissing, their tongues lazily swirling around each other for another ten minutes or so. Mindful that Jeremiah hadn't yet had his release, Asher slowly pulled out of the warm passageway. He reached down and wiped the remnants of his seed off of his still semi-erect member and then used it to lubricate his own hole. Standing up, Asher moved over Jeremiah's midsection and then squatted down onto Jeremiah's erection. He felt the agreeable sensation of the thick head pressing against his entrance, which was shortly followed by that wonderful sense of being stretched and opened up, as the cock pushed deeper inside. His recent ejaculation had made the passageway even more sensitive and Asher took his time to adjust to the solid manhood, as miniature electric shocks ran through his body. Once his buttocks were resting flush against Jeremiah's hips, he contracted and released his well-trained ass muscles, milking the solid member inside of him. With Jeremiah's hands gripping his hips, Asher began to bounce up and down, causing both lads to grunt and groan their pleasure. Asher adored having sex outdoors; the sun heating their skin and the breeze flowing over them excited him to no end. Their bodies having dried from swimming had now become slick with perspiration, and both lads were breathing heavily.

Desperately trying not to think about the fact that it was the last time they would ever lie with one another, tears threatened to wet Asher's eyes but he pushed the emotion down and concentrated on making this time their most intense sexual experience yet. It didn't take long before Asher's experienced maneuvers had their desired effect. Beneath him, Jeremiah's well-built body tensed up and started to shake. Moments later, Asher felt the throbbing of release, as Jeremiah came inside him. Asher was so worked up that he also spurted another torrent of cum, this time all over Jeremiah's heaving chest. Asher collapsed forward; Jeremiah still buried to the hilt and fell back into the gentle kissing once more.

Only ten minutes later, Asher felt Jeremiah hardening inside him again, so he leaned back and gleefully rode it to ejaculation once more. The pair played on and off for the rest of the afternoon, and well into the night, occasionally stopping to frolic in the water or eat something to keep up their energy.

The sun long gone, they began to fall asleep in their tree house, naked in each other's arms, as a soft breeze caressed their bodies. One last regretful thought crossed Asher's mind before sleep properly took hold.

I wish we could just stay like this forever.

* * *

Asher awoke as dawn's first light was beginning to seep through the trees, and coating their bodies in warming shades of orange. It was at that moment, watching Jeremiah peacefully slumber that Asher began to seriously doubt his plan to leave. Even though he had decided a month ago, he had been wavering as the day finally approached. Topher had been wonderful, offering many sympathetic words and encouragement but more and more Asher was feeling like a coward. Absentmindedly, Asher fingered the arrowhead dangling from his necklace, as familiar arguments swirled about his brain.

He's the love of my life, how can I leave him? But if I stay we'll most likely keep fucking and I don't want to be an adulterer. I should be stronger than that. Think of his future…and mine. I have to go.

Just then he was disturbed by the sound of Jeremiah's alarm, which was set early enough to give them time to get home and prepare themselves for the wedding.

"Morning, Ash," murmured Jeremiah, his voice thick with sleep. "You're the best thing to wake up to."

"You, too." Ash tried to keep the misery out of his voice but a thin sliver managed to sneak in. "Not any more though."

Sitting up, Jeremiah took Asher into his arms, pulling him in close.

"I'm so sorry. I wish it could be another way."

"I know." Asher valiantly fought the urge to cry and simply whispered into Jeremiah's ear. "Me, too."

Later that morning, Asher hastily packed the belongings he couldn't bear to be without – some clothes and a handful of his favorite books – into his car. As he loaded the last bag into the backseat, a pang of guilt crossed his heart.

I wish I could tell him that I'm leaving but he'd probably convince me to stay. It's better this way.

The idea of grinning and pretending to be happy for his best friend in the weeks following the nuptials, when the talk in the town would be nothing but the wedding, the honeymoon and how soon they could expect children, was utterly repellent to him. He also felt guilty about leaving so abruptly and closing the library without any notice, although he was sure a suitable replacement would be found without a great deal of trouble.

The plan was to leave that night, after the reception and drive away without saying a word. He could make his apologies to family and friends when he was safely away in Port Davinica, as he knew that if he tried to say goodbye to his sister or mother that he might very well lose his nerve and not be able to go through with it. They had almost as much emotional sway over Asher as Jeremiah.

Looking at his watch, Asher realized that he had less time that he'd thought so he hurried back inside to shave, shower, put his wedding suit on and head on over to the church. In a way, it was better that he was caught up in getting ready as it didn't give him time to reflect further about the momentous life-changing action he was about to make.

No chance to change my mind. I'm making the right decision...aren't I?

* * *

After arriving at the church and giving a warm greeting to his mother and sister, and receiving a dry, formal handshake from his father, Asher took his place by Jeremiah, finding it hard to look at his best friend in the eye.

"You, OK?" whispered Jeremiah.

Asher nodded curtly and did his best to keep himself under control. The guests were soon seated and the bridal march began to play. Asher had to admit that as Agnes walked down the aisle she did make a beautiful bride. She had chosen a flattering cut that while displayed her generous cleavage, downplayed the wideness of her hips and instead of a fluffy meringue she looked more like a princess.

Stealing away my Prince. That wanton harpy!

Silently scolding himself for his uncharitable thoughts, Asher kept himself calm with thoughts of driving away and reuniting with his cousin.

The ceremony proceeded normally and was nearly at its completion. Despite his fears, Asher had managed to get through it without breaking down into hysterics. They had now reached one of the most important parts of the service – one that Asher had been dreading for days.

"Does anyone here, know of any reason why these two people should not be joined in the bonds of holy matrimony?" demanded the Preacher. "Speak now or forever hold your peace."

I do! I'm in love with the groom and he's in love with me! We should be the ones getting married!

Fighting his almost overpowering impulse to scream out his thoughts, Asher remained deathly quiet. The silence was only interrupted by a few coughs and the sound of a fussing baby trying to be placated by its desperate mother in one of the back pews.

After the customary pause the Preacher began to launch into the next section.

"Do you Agnes Elizabeth…"

The wooden doors at the entrance to the church were suddenly flung open, banging against the walls and creating an awful din.

"STOP!"

The Preacher halted and the entire congregation, Asher included, turned towards the source of the interruption to see the town mechanic, Zeke, standing in the doorway. He was dressed in his customary outfit of torn blue jeans, a tight black t-shirt with the sleeves rolled up, highlighting his tattooed arms, looking every inch the bad boy that town gossip made him out to be. His thick black hair was arranged wildly upon his head and his piercing green eyes were a little glassy, presumably from the whiskey he'd been drinking that was now reeking from his pores. He advanced up the aisle, to the mutters and murmurs of the shocked onlookers.

"Agnes, you can't do this, Baby! You know we belong together! Please, come with me now."

For her part, Agnes looked well and truly conflicted. There had been some rumors about her and the strapping mechanic but that had all stopped with her engagement to Jeremiah.

"Listen here, young man, you can't just…" began the Preacher, his face full of righteous anger.

"Shut it, Preacher! Come on, Agnes let's go."

"Zeke, you damn fool, what the blazes are you doing? We talked about this!"

In spite of her harsh tone and words, Agnes looked like she desperately wanted to run off with the handsome mechanic.

"You were with this ruffian, Agnes?" demanded the Preacher. "Jeremiah, aren't you going to say anything?"

"Actually, I am," declared Jeremiah, moving forward to Agnes. "If you love him you should go with him. You have my blessing. In fact, take the tickets for our honeymoon and enjoy it together."

All around the church there were shocked faces, frantic whispers and a general ambiance of confusion and upheaval. In all the town's history there hadn't been a scene like it. For her part, Agnes looked as if she may faint from happiness.

"Thanks, but…but why?"

"Because I know what it's like to be pushed into marrying someone you don't love. I shouldn't be up here with you today. I should be up here with one I truly love." He turned away from Agnes and towards his best man and bent down on one knee. "Asher. I'm sorry it took me so long to get the balls to do this. I don't have a ring to give you, but will you marry me?"

What had been only low rumblings in the crowd became a fully-fledged ruckus at the groom's proclamation of love for his best man and subsequent proposal.

Asher was as stunned as everyone else. He never expected that it would be Jeremiah that would out them, let alone to practically the entire town.

"Is this true?" thundered Asher's father.

Finding courage that he didn't know he possessed, Asher finally stood up to his father.

"Yes, Sir. We're in love."

"I won't have it! No son of mine will be a sodomite! Asher, repent for your wicked ways or you'll be damned for all eternity."

Screw this. I deserve to be happy too!

"No."

"What do you mean, no?"

"Don't make the same mistake as Uncle Hank and Aunt Rosario made with Topher." Asher cast a scathing look to his aunt and uncle seated in the second row. "I'm an adult and I make my own decisions. You can either accept me the way I am or lose me from your life. I love you all dearly but Jeremiah is my future. We're going away for a little while, to give you all some time to think."

"Please, don't," cried Asher's mother. "Don't do this."

"I'm sorry, but it's something we need to do."

Asher saw in his sister's face something approaching awe, even if her eyes were shiny with the start of tears. Jeremiah's parents also stood to voice their protest but he simply waved them off.

Taking Jeremiah's hand, Asher led him out of the church, followed closely behind by Agnes and Zeke, as the assembled guests broke into an even louder chorus of confusion, outrage and gleeful delight at the scandal. Once outside, the two couples faced one another, all appearing a tad shell-shocked.

"Thanks so much, Jeremiah," gushed Agnes. "You too, Asher. I hope you'll be very happy together. I was only really doing it to please my parents; like you, I guess."

"Yeah, guys. Thanks. You dudes are way braver than I am." Zeke gave both the boys bear hugs. "I needed a whole bottle before I could come to my senses and fight for what was right."

"No; thank you," said Jeremiah. "You made me realize what's most important."

"Enjoy Canada!" added Asher.

The former bride-to-be and her mechanic beau hurried off to his waiting mustang and soon peeled out of the town in a spray of dirt. Jeremiah turned to Asher his eyes burning bright with happiness.

"So, where are we going to go?"

"Actually, I was already planning to leave town and stay with Topher in Port Davinica after your wedding," admitted Asher sheepishly. "Don't be mad."

"You were just going to go without telling me?"

"Yes, I'm sorry. It was all too hard. Please forgive me."

A tense few seconds ensued as a range of emotions flitted over Jeremiah's handsome features, before they settled back onto a look of kindness.

"Of course. I would've been hurt, but I do understand. Although none of that matters now. We're going to be together."

By this time, the wedding guests had started to exit the church, the lads' families among them, so they beat a hasty retreat in the direction of the library to get Asher's car.

* * *

Driving fast, the twosome headed straight to Jeremiah's to hurriedly collect some clothes and get the hell out of town, half-afraid of the town forming some sort of hunting party to capture and forcibly convert them back to the status quo. To be fair, it wasn't beyond the realms of possibility, but at least the mob would have been divided as to which of the couples to follow.

Once inside the house, Jeremiah rushed around like a madman, while Asher looked on anxiously, eager to help but not wanting to get in the way. Luckily, Jeremiah had already packed for his honeymoon so he only needed to add some more clothes and a few keepsakes to his luggage before he was ready to go.

Within ten minutes they were back in the car and about to depart. Asher went to turn the key in the ignition when Jeremiah put his hand on top of Asher's stopping him.

"Wait a sec."

Oh, God. He's changed his mind! I knew it was too fantastic to be real.

"What?" The fear of losing everything threatened to overwhelm Asher completely, causing his voice to tremble. "What's the matter?"

"You know, you never answered my question."

"Huh?"

A sly smile crept over Jeremiah's lips as he moved in closer and put his hand on Asher's thigh.

"The one I asked in the church."

Asher's pulse began to slow down again as he realized what Jeremiah wanted to know.

"Oh that?" Asher paused just long enough for Jeremiah's smile to falter before continuing. "Of course, I want to marry you, you doofus!"

They came together and kissed passionately, reigniting their fervent carnal urges. Forgetting their hurry, their hands began to pull at each other's clothing and might have continued further if Asher's phone hadn't started to ring – for the twentieth time since they left the church...Jeremiah had already turned his off before the wedding. Checking the display, he saw that it was his father. A powerful sense of regret and sadness flooded through his heart as he switched off his phone.

"We really have to go."

They hightailed it out of the driveway sending a plume of dust up in their wake. Less than five minutes later, they were approaching the town limits and the weather-beaten sign that Asher had passed many times before.

YOU'RE NOW LEAVING MAGNOLIA FALLS

DON'T BE A STRANGER!

Suddenly, Asher felt a strange clutching in his throat, forcing him to abruptly pull over to the side of the road.

"Are you OK?" asked an anxious-looking Jeremiah. "What's wrong?"

"I…I just want to make sure that this is what you really want. Once we leave it may be a long time before we can come back. I don't want you to have any regrets."

"Surer than anything in my life. The only regret I have is that I didn't stand up to my family sooner. If I can't have you then I don't want anything else. Not the damn orchard or my close-minded family. Besides, I'm pretty sure I already burnt my bridges back at the church."

Overcome with emotion, Asher leaned forward and drew Jeremiah into a hungry embrace. A few minutes passed and the pair reluctantly parted once more.

"More of that when we get to the city."

"Damn Skippy!" agreed Jeremiah, his face practically beaming with joy. "Hope your cousin has soundproof walls."

"We'll have to be on our best behavior…to start with, anyway."

Putting the car into gear, Asher maneuvered back onto the road and they rapidly built up speed, leaving a thoroughly stunned town in their wake.

Twenty miles later they reached the turn off to the freeway that led straight to Port Davinica. Once on the freeway, Asher felt himself relax even more. As the landscape whizzed past, Asher tried not to think of the life he was leaving behind but of the brand new one he was embarking on. A few hours later, the sun had begun its descent, bathing the car and its occupants in a soothing amber glow. Up ahead in the distance, the twinkling lights of the city started to appear, growing in number as darkness fell and they sped ever closer towards their destination. Even though they were heading into an uncertain future, Asher felt himself smiling like the proverbial Cheshire Cat. Turning towards Jeremiah, Asher saw that he also wore a matching grin of contentment.

Who knows what'll happen? But at least we'll face it together.

ABOUT THE AUTHOR

Jimi could be considered to be something of a refined blend of Australian/Polish heritage – given his passion for the arts, vodka and BBQs. He now lives in Paris with his wonderfully understanding French husband and cats.

For other of his raunchy ramblings and published work, feel free to browse http://www.jimify.me follow him on Twitter & Instagram @jimifyme or show your devotion at facebook.com/JIMIFY.ME

DIGITAL TITLES BY JIMI GONINAN

For all Jimi's titles please visit his page at lydianpress.com

IN PRINT FROM LYDIAN PRESS

DOM'S DELIGHTS

Come on in and taste the love!

Dom has worked hard pursuing his dreams of delighting the masses with his tasty treats - indeed his cream has been eagerly eaten all about the town. Now he has almost everything he ever dreamed of – a successful business, loving friends and a beautiful beau. There's just one more thing he needs to make his life complete...to finally marry the man of his dreams!

BEST SERVED HOT

Revenge has never been sweeter.

When Jameson loses everything he holds dear, he almost drowns in a sea of despair. Bitter and broken, he shuns his friends and retreats from the world. Then a chance encounter with a handsome young man offers him a glimmer of hope, and he slowly begins to piece his life back together. Will he be given the second chance at the love he so desperately deserves?

A MAN FOR EVERY OCCASION

There's always time for love.

The bustling city of Port Davinica is home to many stories of love, lust and more than a few happy endings. Follow the adventures of these men as they find love in all manner of places with an amorous touch of the supernatural thrown in for good measure. You'll soon discover in this collection of romantic tales that no matter the festive occasion – Halloween, Christmas, and especially Valentine's Day - there's always time for love.

THE VIRGIN HEART

Some things are worth waiting for.

Abraham Chadwick is locked in a state of quiet desperation. Not only has he never been kissed, he's never even been in love. Indeed, as Abraham prepares for college, he's beginning to fret that he may stay a virgin forever. Fortunately, the sudden arrival of a handsome Southern gentleman into his world gives him a new sense of hope. Will Abraham finally find the love and affection that he's so desired for so long?

THE MILE HIGH CUB

Serviced with a smile!

Time to buckle up it's going to be a bumpy ride… Flying high with Alex Mathieson, who embraces life as an ever-so-friendly air steward with gay abandon. Until, that is, he falls for a handsome pilot, Peter, and a drastic decision sees him heading into unchartered territory, which may change his life forever.

Lydian Press is dedicated to bringing you the finest
GLBTQ erotic literature on the web.

Visit us on the web at:

http://lydianpress.com